I0756265

FINISHING LINE PRESS
www.finishinglinepress.com

Unknown & Other Stories

by

Barry Vitcov

Finishing Line Press
Georgetown, Kentucky

Unknown & Other Stories

ISBN 979-8-89990-403-5 First Edition

ACKNOWLEDGMENTS

An Unknown Woman	*CafeLit*	December 28, 2022
An Unknown Woman	*Labyrinth*	January 2024
Unknown Parts I - IV	*Mobius Blvd.*	October 2024
Unknown Parts V - VI	*Dark Horses*	August 2025

Publisher: Leah Huete de Maines
Editor: Christen Kincaid
Cover Art: Barry Vitcov
Author Photo: William E. Saltzstein
Cover Design: Elizabeth Maines McCleavy

Order online: www.finishinglinepress.com
also available on amazon.com

Author inquiries and mail orders:
Finishing Line Press
PO Box 1626
Georgetown, Kentucky 40324
USA

Contents

Unknown Stories

For My Grandson
Casey August Sun-Vitcov
Born on Pi Day, 2025

Unknown Stories

Part I
An Unknown Woman

The Pacific is leaning toward the coastline. A full moon casting vibrating light on the breakers, the creaks of seabirds punctuating the light tympani of tides. With a full view, he sits with Beatrice, a nine-year old, black standard poodle, watching a sloop making its way from north to south. He wonders about the sailor's destination while Beatrice patiently waits for another treat. It's been a pleasant day of walking the bluffs, reading the latest Silva thriller, and enjoying the vista with a Knob Creek rye at hand. The mood is broken by a knock at the door and a quick bark from Beatrice who leaps toward the entryway tail wagging and eager to meet whoever is there.

He opens the door to a tall woman with long, black hair and binoculars hanging from her neck. She wears a loose fitting, white linen blouse and black pajama-style pants. She smiles and casually tells him she's late because she was watching whales spout and breach in the bay. She gives him a light peck on the cheek, reaches down and gives Beatrice a playful squeeze behind her left ear, and strides in saying she would soon have dinner on the table. He closes the door, turns and asks, "Who are you?"

She pauses, looks back at him with a smile that dares him to ask again, and suggests that he return to whatever he was already doing while she goes into the kitchen. Beatrice seems unfazed by the woman's appearance; in fact, is accepting of her affectionate gesture. He has always trusted Beatrice's instinct toward novelty, so he returns to his leather chair without a thought for the peculiar nature of what was happening. He resumes his attention to his whiskey and the view of the ocean. He is a writer by profession, a dreamer by nature, and a seeker of harmless adventure. He takes a sip of rye and waits patiently for whatever may ensue while Beatrice curls at his feet.

Minutes later cooking sounds and smells emerge from the kitchen. The fragrance of onion and garlic with the sizzle of sautéing ground beef fills the air with familiarity and he thinks a sauce is being made, perhaps a Bolognese to go with some fresh pappardelle pasta he had recently purchased at the Italian deli in town. The refrigerator door opens several times and there is crack of lettuce being torn and the clack of a knife cutting other produce. He figures she must be making a salad. She calls from the kitchen saying dinner won't be long and he should open a bottle of good red wine and set the dining room table with a salad plate and bowl for pasta. He's pleased with his knowing.

Beatrice alerts him to a flock of gulls swooping low over the shoreline. She's shown an interest in birdlife since early puppyhood. Fortunately, her incessant barking as a young pup has matured into a low growl and single yelp whenever sighting any of the many birds who make their home in Sea Ranch. He pushes himself up from his chair, walks to the dining room, with Beatrice at his side, where wine is stored in a climate-controlled closet and chooses a zinfandel from the Dry Creek terroir. He opens the drawer at the end of the table, removes placemats, retrieves plain white bowls, salad plates, and cutlery from a sideboard and sets the table for two. He uncorks the wine and places a couple of Riedel wine glasses beside the place settings. She calls out from the kitchen to thank him for having San Marzano tomatoes in the pantry and that dinner is only minutes away. He knows it will be at least another thirty minutes before the sauce has a chance to develop and mellow its distinctive flavor, so he pours himself another Knob Creek and settles back to watching the ocean. Beatrice looks at him with a cock of her head and slightly raised ears before curling at his feet without any verbal comment.

As he expected, a simple dinner of pasta a la Bolognese and green salad lightly dressed with a vinaigrette expertly made with olive oil, lemon, minced garlic, salt and pepper. They sit without saying a word. Beatrice finds her regular spot under the table and safely away from pesky feet that might disturb her own dinner dreams. Having allowed this beautiful, unknown woman into his home felt like a reverie, a story conjured from his overly active imagination. He looked into her jade green eyes before filling the wine glasses and taking a bite of pasta and commenting, "One of the best I've ever had. Where did you learn to cook?"

She lifted her glass toward him with a suggestive look and answered, "Here and there."

He had once read a short story where two strangers met in a coffee shop, ended up spending several hours over espressos before leaving for his beachside apartment and an unforgettable one-night stand. They had never learned each other's names and said goodbye after post-coital lattes at the same coffee shop where they began an inexplicable fantasy. The story enchanted him with its improbability and eroticism. He often wondered if such a scenario were really possible or just the lustful thoughts of male libido.

He asked, "Did you walk far?"

"You already know the answer," she replied with the smile of an enchantress.

The fiction he had read involved gorgeous people. Like the woman sitting at his table, she was tall with long dark hair and jade green eyes. The man in the story was also tall with a well-proportioned body and an athletic walk. Unlike the man in the story, he has no athletic ability, is tall with poor posture, unstylish reddish-brown hair beginning to gray at the temples, and a face blotchy with freckles. He doesn't drink espressos or lattes and has difficulty carrying on a conversation for more than a few minutes. His friends describe him as shy with a receding personality. The redundancy is unfortunately appropriate. He's thinking he must be the victim of an elaborate practical joke.

With every bite of Bolognese and sip of wine, he becomes both more curious and comfortable with the situation. He relaxes into a deeper state of ambiguity, in which he is edgy about where this scene is going and yet at ease with this unknown woman's company. Until sitting at the dining table, he felt caught in a visual fog, but now details began to emerge. He notices a small, almost imperceptible, scar on the ridge of her right cheekbone, which acts to highlight her perfect olive complexion. Her fingers are long and elegantly manicured and painted magenta. The few words she's uttered remind him of what he imagines a Southern belle might sound like, a slight musical drawl but without the blond hair. She sits with perfect posture, slowly savoring the meal she prepared. How did she know what was in his kitchen and where to find the necessary cooking gear?

"Just visiting Sea Ranch?" he asks.

"You might say that."

When he was a boy growing up in San Francisco, he became a fan of a group of jugglers who regularly performed in Golden Gate Park. Every Saturday at noon, a VW bus brightly painted in a psychedelic motif parked near the panhandle and six jugglers emerged. Three men dressed as clowns and three women in harem outfits, sporting pierced navels and bodies that moved like octopuses. They loudly drew attention with poor puns, dry wit, and skillful juggling with an assortment of objects. He watched for the entire hour's performance savoring the encore when flaming batons were tossed back and forth without a care for personal safety. The only miscue was when a tossed knife nicked the cheek of one of the woman jugglers causing a gasp from the observers and indifference from the performers. The crowd that had gathered broke into hoots and applause and filled the juggler's hats with coin and paper money after the show. He thought it was a great way to earn a living and tried for months to teach himself how to juggle. Unfortunately, his lack of coordination led to many broken plates and bruised fruit and he abandoned all hope of being a performer. Instead, he used the experience to write a series of stories about a troupe of traveling jugglers who popped up unannounced at parks across the country. Those stories eventually became a ten-volume set of bestselling young adult books affording him the luxury of living at Sea Ranch. He remembered that one of the women jugglers looked very much like the woman sitting before him.

Dinner continued without conversation until Beatrice stood, walked over to the woman and placed her shaved muzzle on her right thigh. The woman looked down at Beatrice, put her fork on the edge of her plate like a well-mannered sophisticate, and reached down to scratch Beatrice behind both ears. Beatrice had a way of developing relationships whether ongoing or temporary. The woman smiled at Beatrice and told her she was a sweet girl. Beatrice reacted to the compliment with all the nonchalance of a well-schooled debutante.

"Beatrice doesn't like everybody," commented the man.

She said, "I have a way with dogs."

The first glasses of wine were finished and another poured. Dinner was also finished and the woman stacked the dirty dishes, collected the used silverware, and took them to the kitchen. She directed, "Wait here, we'll have dessert."

He sat savoring the wine. Dry Creek was a region not far from Sea Ranch. It was famous for lush vineyards and world-class wines, especially its zinfandels and cabernet sauvignons. He kept a good selection in his wine closet but rarely had the opportunity to share a bottle and certainly not share a bottle with a woman who mysteriously shows up, enters his home with hardly a word, and makes a fabulous meal, which they eat in relative silence. Who is this woman? Why did he allow her into his home? Did this bode for a tragic ending? Were there compatriots waiting outside to storm his home, cause bodily harm, and steal whatever they might find? And what could she possibly be offering for dessert?

She returns with two dishes of ice cream. He forgot about the unopened quart of spumoni in his freezer. He had purchased it several months ago at the market in Gualala and now it was being served after a delicious Italian dinner. Coincidence? Planning? None of what was happening made any sense. Beatrice was fond of spumoni. There were no other foods she would beg for, but now she sat at the stranger's side faithfully waiting for the icy treat. Without asking him permission, she scooped some of the ice cream with her forefinger and offered it to Beatrice, who happily licked it and sat waiting for more.

It suddenly dawned on him that this woman might be an employee at the grocery store and maybe that's the connection. "Beatrice has made a lifelong friend," he said. "By any chance, do you work at the Surf?"

"She's a sweet girl. No, I don't work."

He wanted to ask the most important question, "Who are you and what are you doing here?" but didn't want to break the mood or the spell he seemed to be under. Between the two Knob Creeks and two glasses of zinfandel, he was feeling warm, cozy, and safe in this woman's presence. Beatrice continued to approve of the woman while consuming most of her dish of ice cream as it was offered finger scoop by finger scoop. He had not eaten any of his spumoni and it had melted into a gob of dried fruit, nuts, and a pool of watery gelato and whipped cream.

She suggested taking their wine and going to the living room. He sat back in his maroon leather chair cradling his goblet, as she on the matching sofa across from him. He did not want to be so forward as to sit next to her. They both had views of the ocean, which, in a full moon's light appeared magical with lit whitecaps and shadowy tides. They sat quietly for almost thirty minutes. Beatrice jumped up on the sofa and snuggled against the woman's hip. Beatrice had no problem being forward.

Finally, the woman broke the silence. “I once read a story about a beautiful, dark-haired member of a traveling troupe of jugglers. One day she met a handsome man at a coffee shop where they drank espressos, talked for hours, and had a torrid love affair without ever sharing identities. It’s the strangest story I ever read.”

“I believe I know what you mean,” replied the man.

Part II
The Woman Unknown

The Sea Ranch stretches ten miles along the Sonoma County coastline, the Pacific Ocean a tidal reminder of contemplative mystery. Monterey cypress along the ocean bluffs, like sentinels calling a halt to the continent, punctuate imagination. Miles of trails meander among open meadows with vegetation kept at bay by hundreds of sheep moved about by two skilled sheepherders, who work alone without a crook, dogs or any other assistance.

The community's architectural design requires sameness and a blending into the natural environment. Angular construction, shades of browns and greys, and natural wood siding determine the uniqueness of each structure. Less than a third are occupied by permanent residents, artists, writers, remote workers and others seeking a solitary lifestyle. Many are one-percenters who own houses as status symbols, like expensive jewelry that serves no purpose except to impress. Some are primarily used as vacation rental homes, an easy form of passive income for those who enjoy flaunting passivity as a virtue with an easy return on investment.

Mail must always be addressed to The Sea Ranch, never Sea Ranch without the capitalized determiner. It is The pronounced thee. Without pretense, there wouldn't be The Sea Ranch. It's the American dream of royalty without blood legacy.

I've lived here since the early days, a refugee from city life lucky enough to have purchased a lot and built one of the most modest of homes near the bluffs with clear views of the ocean and the house closest to mine, one with better ocean views and a quiet, more well-to-do owner. Technology enabled me to keep my job as an editor for a large publishing house, which specializes in supernatural fiction. Coincidentally, my neighbor is a successful writer of young adult fiction and an inveterate walker with his standard poodle. We are what might be called "nodding neighbors" because, beyond initial introductions, our only form of communication is a nod and an occasional word or two about the weather or other mundane news. Everything else I've learned about him came from Google or observation, with and without a good set of Nikon binoculars.

I learned from the Internet his occupation, published works, approximate wealth, political donations (he identifies as a progressive with strong affiliations to environmental causes) and no living relatives. My observations indicate few visitors, which I suppose means few friends, and the odd habit of practicing, or should I say attempting, to juggle fruit. Every afternoon, rain, shine, wind, or dense fog, he appears in his unfenced front yard with limes, lemons, oranges, sometimes even bananas, and tries to juggle. Always with no success and lots of bruised fruit left to rot or be consumed at night by grateful racoons. He is one of the least coordinated men I have ever seen. I have no idea why he has such an obsession with juggling other than the fact that his books are about a troupe of successful jugglers.

I once read one of his books just to get a better idea of my neighbor's proclivity for juggling. The jugglers in his books risk life and limb juggling all sorts of dangerous objects: knives, chain saws, flaming torches, poisonous snakes. Never fruit, unless it involves a knife and the magical paring of an apple. I worried that one day he would try such a perilous feat with horrific results and I would have to call 9ll.

At least three times a week he drives into town to purchase fruit to juggle and other groceries. I always hear him leaving because his green Morgan Roadster has a distinct rumble as he crunches along the gravel driveway leading to the asphalt roadway and then gives the car a little extra juice and squeals off with a honk. I'm convinced he knows I'm watching and enjoys marking the occasion with a flamboyant touch. I find it amusing that he doesn't give a little salute from his tweed driving cap.

He never returns with less than three grocery bags filled with an abundance of gourmet foods. I only know this because on more than one occasion he has dropped a bag…he is an uncoordinated man, after all…and I've seen their contents. Fancy tomatoes from Italy, tuna fish in a jar, a variety of locally foraged mushrooms, oils and vinegars and spices and herbs purchased in the ethnic foods section, hot sauces galore, and vegetables like escarole and bok choy, which few regular folk eat. I know these things because I'm a bit of a foodie myself and there is only one market in town that carries those items. He also happens to be a fan of Knob Creek rye whiskey, which he purchases by the case. I enjoy a nip or two of sherry or brandy, especially on cool, foggy nights, but he appears to have a more regular habit. I'm not suggesting he's an alcoholic. I would never make that accusation.

I would, however, suggest that he is a bit of a romantic. He's not a man whose looks draw attention. Frumpy might be the best word to describe him. Yet, he drives an eye-catching sports car, wears a jaunty cap and leather driving gloves behind the wheel and has a standard poodle. His young adult fiction uses the nomadic and often romantic juggler's lives as a basis for lusty teenage romance. Yes, he's a romantic at heart.

I realize it is a cliché to open a tale with 'on a dark and stormy night' but this did happen on a dark and stormy night, although I may be imagining the dark and stormy part. It just seemed that way, the way some things seem when nothing makes sense. And that particular night did not make sense. How could a woman walk into a house, a beautiful, tall woman with long dark hair, dressed with an air of casual elegance, binoculars hanging loosely from her neck, a woman I had never seen before, walk into a house and never leave.

Before I moved to The Sea Ranch, I was accused of falsely imprisoning a woman. It was all a huge misunderstanding that involved interviewing a potential dog sitter for my apricot miniature poodle, Attitude. It was the perfect name for her because, like most miniature poodles, she had an inflated sense of entitlement and size. She believed she was a large dog who could move people around like a herding dog, a Shetland Sheepdog or Australian Shepherd. In other words, Attitude, Addie for short, was a head-butter. It's another coincidence that my neighbor happens to have a standard poodle, who apparently is not that entitled. I cook for Addie, boiled chicken, the leanest ground beef I can find, expensive fish…halibut, rock cod…and mix it with grains and supplements. She won't go anywhere near kibble, canned food, or any commercial product labeled dog food. Her treats are either bits of Hebrew National hotdogs…raises her nose at Oscar Mayer… or string cheese. My neighbor's dog eats Purina and Milk-Bones, delivered in bulk from Chewy.com.

I did not work remotely when I lived in San Francisco, and Addie's current dog walker had given a one-month notice that she was moving. One late afternoon, I was interviewing this nice young woman, who claimed to be a professional dog walker and sitter. I asked if she'd like something to drink… tea, water, juice, soft drink…while we chatted. She said tea would be nice, and I went to the kitchen to make a pot. I always keep a variety of teas from Red Blossom Tea Company, and, based on her youthful appearance and time of the day, decided to brew a pot of peppermint tea. She asked to use the bathroom, and I pointed to a door down the hall. I neglected to tell her not to use the lock because it had a notorious habit of sticking and trapping whoever was inside.

Brewing tea is a process that takes time. I was in the kitchen puttering about, arranging a small collection of Pepperidge Farm cookies on a plate and setting up a serving tray with cups and saucers. Long story short, the woman was locked in the bathroom, panicked and used her cell phone to call the police. She never even attempted to rap on the door, call out, or do anything a normal, mature person would do. The excuse she offered was that she had once been locked in a room by a prospective client who did intend harm. She escaped after a tussle, reported it to the authorities who told her she was being silly and overly reactive.

The two female officers who showed up at my house listened to her allegation and suggested she should consider work in a more public space. After she left, one of the officers pulled me aside and said it was never a good idea for a man to interview a woman, a total stranger, alone in their home. Point well taken, and my next interview was held at a local bakery over coffee.

From that incident, I realized how easy life experience influences perceptions and how our own biases are a product of our past. This is why I want to be extra careful about the tale I'm about to share. The dark and stormy night cliché was more a state of my mind. The reality being it was a clear and fairly calm night. I had been keeping watch on the ocean and my neighbor's house, and, unlike my neighbor who was probably enjoying a Knob Creek whiskey while sitting with his dog, I sat with a snifter of Remy Martin in hand and Addie standing alert at my side. I don't buy the most expensive or the cheapest brandy. The Remy Martin I enjoy has a nice sweetness and heat. My window was wide open so that I could hear waves breaking against the bluff and smell the briny mist in the air.

There was a full moon, clear skies, a flat ocean, and a small two-masted sailboat easing its way to a nearby port. Out of nowhere a woman walked up to my neighbor's front door. She simply appeared like a specter. If there had been a thick fog that night, which is normal at The Sea Ranch, her arrival out of a mist would have made sense. There was no misty shroud. There was no car, no Uber or taxi, signaling her arrival. There was no bike, although that would have been odd because few cycle for transportation at The Sea Ranch. I don't believe in extra-terrestrials, but the thought did occur to me that her form of transport might very well have been alien in nature. Her surreal beauty suggested a certain unworldliness.

She knocked and I heard a single bark from my neighbor's poodle.

Addie never gave single barks. In fact, she only barks at birds, quails being her bird of choice. The door opened, the woman entered and never reappeared. I sat well past midnight keeping watch. My neighbor's house has no windows facing mine. I could only watch his front door for signs of life or any other activity. There was none. I fell asleep in my chair after a second round of brandy and was awakened by Addie's barking, her 6:00 a.m. signal that it was time for a morning walk. It's interesting how dogs tell time. I once heard an expert on dog behavior suggest that dogs tell time with their noses. It's amazing what dogs can do, from sit, stay, fetch, rollover, and diagnose certain cancers. Might Addie be able to help solve the mystery of the unknown woman who entered my neighbor's house and never reappeared? I realize you might be thinking she left while I was sleeping. I doubt that. And I don't think I'm overreacting. Certainly, not after I confronted my neighbor while out walking Addie.

I'm not a man with much machismo. I detest violence of any sort, can't bear to watch boxing matches, football, rugby, or any other game that reeks of men trying to prove how manly they are. I'm a gentle sort with a slight build and a sweet tenor voice. Despite my far-from-brutish appearance, I have a strong verbal presence when I need to be assertive.

Addie and I were walking the trail along the bluff and stopped to watch a flock of brown pelicans diving and fishing. It was like watching a comical, helter-skelter dance that turns into a gracefully choreographed ballet. Our reverie was interrupted when the neighbor and his standard poodle walked toward us, his poodle sniffing the ground and he with a nod. I nodded back and in that instant decided it was time for conversation but, before I could say anything, he spoke.

"Good morning," he said with a smile that indicated he might be hiding something. "How was your evening?"

"Just fine," I replied. "And yours."

"Unexpected and different."

I'm not much for cryptic dialogue, so I risked asking what made the evening a surprise. He said that sometimes things happen that can't be explained, 'marvelous things, special things, life-changing things.'

"Usually, that involves a woman," I said.

"Yes," he said before walking away with a little extra spring to his gait.

Addie looked up at me with a what-the-hell-was-that-all-about expression. You know, the kind where your dog cocks her head with a bemused look in her eyes. And that's when I decided to be more direct.

I called out, "I saw an unknown woman enter your house last night."

"Did you, now?"

"I did but never saw her leave."

"You must have a very vivid imagination," he said. "No one came to my house last night."

That was all I needed to know. He continued to walk away, and I walked back. Before going into my house, I stopped and knocked hard on his door. No one answered. I knocked harder and called out asking if everything was okay inside. Still, no answer. I thought back to my own experience with a false accusation. I decided this was different. I used my cell phone to call The Sea Ranch security. They arrived shortly along with a sheriff's deputy.

I explained my concern, the deputy directed me to return to my house while they waited for my neighbor. More than an hour passed before the deputy came to my door. She explained that the interview with the neighbor yielded no concern. At the neighbor's invitation, she was allowed to inspect the house and found no evidence of any wrongdoing.

"Your neighbor told us he had a quiet evening at home. He said he ate dinner alone and had a nice Bolognese pasta, simple green salad, and fine local wine. The dishes in his sink confirmed only dinner for one.

I think you must have been mistaken. Perhaps, a bit under the influence of that bottle of brandy I see over there on the coffee table."

The deputy's suggestion angered me. Fortunately, I'm able to remain stoic in the face of outrage. I firmly responded by informing her that I did not drink to excess and that I know what I saw. I suggested a clever coverup by my neighbor. The deputy listened without comment, thanked me for my concern, and left. She confided something to the security person, who shook his head, and then they both drove off.

I sat in my watcher's chair. Addie sat next to me before curling and drifting off to one of her many naps. Fog began drifting ashore, gossamer-like fingers grasping at the landscape. I began to enter my own dreamlike slumber. I felt the tension in my shoulders and a general sense of unease flowing away. When I opened my eyes, it was dark with fog completely blocking any view I had of the ocean or my neighbor's house.

There was a gentle knock at my door. Addie gave a short bark, which was odd because she only barks at birds. I answered the door and standing there was a tall woman with long, black hair and binoculars hanging from her neck. She was wearing a loose fitting, white linen blouse and black pajama-style pants. She smiled and casually told me that she was late because she was watching whales spout and breach in the bay. She gave me a light peck on the cheek, reached down and gave Addie a playful squeeze behind her left ear, and strode in saying she would soon have dinner on the table. I closed the door, turned and asked, "Who are you?"

Part III
Known Woman Unknown

'I live in the hearts and minds of many. I am whatever you need me to be. Vermeer and Renoir painted me. Sinatra sang about me. Software developers used my virtual likeness when developing their games. I have an age and I am ageless. Mortality will never pay a visit. I am part of your history; I am part of everyone's experience. My gender is in your mind, not mine. I arrive like fog and capture your imagination. I was born into a troupe of jugglers and was raised to appreciate and practice the art of deception. I am a writer's conjuration.'

That is what she told me as I sat watching a two-masted sloop make its way to port. Every night before dinner, I sit in my Mission style leather chair enjoying a Knob Creek rye watching the sea. My black standard poodle Beatrice curled at my feet. It's the structured time of each day when I write in my Moleskine journal using my favorite Pilot fountain pen. I'm a writer and I require routine. I write five pages every morning and allocate one-hour to journal each evening. No exceptions. No excuses. Write or die.

There's an old adage that writers should write what they know. I've always felt that would be terribly limiting to one's imagination. Writers ought to be like explorers seeking new lands, new solutions, new opportunities. The only limitations are vocabulary, energy and time. Experience does not hinder; in fact, it only helps to adjust those three limitations.

Vocabulary, which can be used to impress, does not need to be vast. Think of vocabulary as a set of piano keys. A grand piano has eighty-eight keys, which can be arranged to play an untold number of symphonies. Writers can expand or contract vocabulary as necessary to match the reader's needs. Experience builds a basic vocabulary but there are outside resources writers have available when one's own experience is limiting. A dictionary, thesaurus, Google are all easily available. Technology has made words available to everyone. Writers know how to take advantage.

Energy and fitness is more problematic. As much as we try to maintain our youthful vigor, we learn it is on the wane after a first significant illness or when your ophthalmologist informs you it's time for cataract surgery. We start out as runners and become walkers. We stretch and lift weights and still notice sagging skin around our jowls and under our upper arms. We get older and our bodies inevitably change. The one factor that keeps writers from succumbing to the natural loss of energy is desire. The motivation to write is fundamental.

Until recently I thought time was fixed. However, my study of jugglers, magicians, and practitioners of the occult has taught me otherwise. I won't comment on the occult or supernatural, because that could lead to unintended and dire consequences. Magicians don't manipulate time, they play with our perceptions, and we know they are fooling us but we don't care. Jugglers, on the other hand, are capable of luring us into a spectral world where they manipulate our perception of reality through extraordinary performances. The most exceptional jugglers have the capacity to make their audiences suspend belief. How can anyone, working solo or with others, keep multiple objects in motion, afloat, and in synchronicity. Jugglers take us out of our time and into theirs. I've tried juggling for years, mostly with fruit. From time to time, I am able to juggle three apples. I've been told fourteen is the maximum. How do you get from the unattainable three to what I believe is an impossible fourteen? And that's for one juggler! Juggling troupes continuously expand limits and I assert they've combined the talents of magicians (and those occultists I won't mention again) to create new dimensions free of the limitations of time and space. Jugglers are really a practical extension of Einstein's genius. Magicians and jugglers use physical objects to suspend time…sometimes place…and create new experiences, which audiences use words to describe. Is it possible for a writer to use words to suspend time and create new physical spaces? This isn't about writers who use magical realism like Murakami, Chiang, or Allende as an invitation for us to suspend our disbelief and take us into newly imagined worlds. No, I'm suggesting the suspension of firmly held beliefs and the creation of new worlds, not virtual ones.

The first time it happened was on a clear, autumn night in Sea Ranch. I sat with Beatrice watching the ocean, a boat sailing to port, brown pelicans swooping low and diving for fish. Whitecaps bloomed like tiny puffs of fairy dust before the sea became unaccustomedly calm. I made a note in my journal that the "world had stilled, a tiny boat ceased moving, the sea became a mirror to the sky and all who lived there." There was the curious scent of sage and rosemary in the air, yet none grew around the house.

I must have dozed before I heard Beatrice rouse me with a sharp bark at the front door. I took a quick sip of whiskey and glanced at the ocean, which had become active again. The tides slapping heavily against the rocky outcrops throwing mists high, and the sloop much farther south. The odor of sage and rosemary had changed to basil, an herb I always have available when I prepare Italian meals. The remainder of the evening was spent enjoying dinner, wine, and conversation, the kind of conversation reserved for writers who are capable of feeling their own words as though they are tangible objects, and comfortable with gaps in understanding.

I woke early from a deep sleep with no memorable dreams. Beatrice was slow to uncurl from the edge of her bed. She stretched and stood ready to be leashed for her morning walk along the bluffs. She appeared to have thoughts about the previous night but I'm not able to read a dog's mind. I believe dogs have memories that are like locked diaries, never to be opened and shared. For me, the evening was a vague smear. I must have been suffering from selective amnesia. I quickly donned sweats, walking shoes, and a blue watch cap before stopping in the kitchen for a glass of orange juice. The sink contained rinsed dishes, cutlery, and cooking gear from dinner. There were only dishes and glassware for one diner; I thought there should have been for two. I bent to clip the leash to Beatrice's collar and saw a note on the kitchen island. "Thank you," written with a woman's delicate serif.

I saw my neighbor on the trail walking towards us. Beatrice and I are not fond of him or his irritating little dog. I named him The Snoop shortly after our first introduction, and when his miniature poodle made any conversation impossible with her loud, high-pitched barking at the quail skittering among the short, dry grasses. I know he watches us while pretending to whale watch with his outsized nosiness and undersized binoculars. Whenever I leave my house to drive into town and run errands, I see him staring out his front window. I always give the car a little extra jolt, spinning my tires on the gravel drive, while waving goodbye like a celebrity. Fortunately, he can't see inside my house from his. I specifically instructed the architects to design a home that gave me complete indoor privacy from neighbors. I'm sure that frustrates The Snoop.

Out of politeness, I said hello, ignored his irritable, bird-pestering miniature poodle, and walked on by. Beatrice, keeping to her normal regal behavior, held her head and tail high and offered no comment. The Snoop restrained himself for a brief moment before prying. He asked about a woman. Since I wasn't even sure what had happened the previous evening, I chose a nebulous response given with a duplicitous smile, which he could interpret anyway he wanted. I knew he was an editor and therefore lacked imagination.

Shortly after returning home, a Sea Ranch security officer and sheriff's deputy interrupted my pre-breakfast cup of morning coffee with questions and false allegations.

I had nothing to hide and didn't feel it wise to share a virtual, authentic, or parallel reality. I had no certainty about the night in question, so I related the only reality that made sense at the time. Any other reality would be one I would have to resolve on my own. I told them that, to the best of my knowledge, I had spent the night alone, although I did leave out the phrase to the best of my knowledge. I figured that law enforcement could only understand empirical facts, and anything offered as theoretically abstract would be alarming. I allowed them to enter my home and look around. The dishes in the kitchen sink were evidence enough that nothing untoward had occurred in my home. They said they were sorry for the intrusion and departed. I assumed they were headed over to The Snoop's.

My morning writing time had been delayed. I was not happy about the interruption to my routine. After a breakfast of Greek vanilla yogurt with raspberries, a buttered English muffin, and French-pressed black coffee for me and a bowl of Purina for Beatrice, I sat with my laptop computer watching the fog surround Sea Ranch like a preparation for a smoky seance. I smelled sage and rosemary again, with a slight hint of spearmint. I wrote for the remainder of the morning feeling the moodiness of the fog like a cool heavy blanket that brings comfort when trying to fall asleep.

I wrote about a group of women mimes who juggled. They tossed and caught implied objects. The absence of balls, tenpins, knives, small animals, or anything else typically used by jugglers didn't matter to the audience. The audience was comprised of people and their poodles, who were all dressed in colorful costumes. All the people were face-painted and all the poodles wore conical hats. It looked like a Felliniesque gathering. Before each juggling routine, a mime carried a sign across the stage declaring what objects would be juggled. With each routine, the objects became increasingly dangerous. During the knife juggling portion of the show, one woman, a dark-haired beauty, feigned injury. A small cut appeared on her cheek, and she wiped away what appeared to be real blood.

Later that afternoon after a nap without a dream, there was a knock at my door. Beatrice gave a growl and a bark. The signal she reserved for those she is not fond of. I answered and there stood The Snoop with the look of someone who had just experienced euphoria and the need to tell someone.

"Who was she?" he asked.

Part IV
Knowing a Woman

He wasn't from France. He didn't speak French. He found French cuisine an overly indulgent diet. His preferred foods were brisket, latkes, and matzo ball soup. He despised the French but took advantage of a stereotypic image. His prettified accent, turned-up and waxed mustache, and Marcel Marceau costume were not merely smoke and mirrors. It was snake oil and subterfuge, a theatrical flair learned at an early age from his grandparents Earl and Louise Liebowitz, known as the Juggling Hippies, who made a modest living busking on city streets and the occasional circus booking. He didn't deny or apologize for his assumed image and, like his grandparents who combined juggling with wit, he married a phony persona with his gift of humorous gab. When onstage Monsieur Mime frequently broke the third wall and spoke directly to his audience. Being a mime and actively explaining his silent routine was all part of the act. He might interrupt breaking out of an imagined jail cell, turning to the audience and pleading for help to find the hair pin he dropped. "Do I have a volunteer who would be willing to come on stage and retrieve what I just dropped? I need it to pick this lock," he would announce with his overly fake and smarmy accent. "And please bring a twenty-dollar bill with you to pay bail after you've been arrested for aiding and abetting a jailbreak." He collected the cash, completed the act, and bowed to a smattering of applause. In reality, he was a below average mime with a questionable reputation. He managed to find work because of his persuasive skills and the ability to collect on chits won from after-hour poker games. Despite his kitsch and lack of talent, he had a flair for discovering new talent. When he wasn't Monsieur Mime, he was Marvin Leibowitz. He had a well-earned reputation as a talent agent. It was a gorgeous, dark-haired woman who walked into his office one afternoon who changed his life. She claimed to be the daughter of jugglers.

His first impression, once he put aside her beauty, was the sense that she was there and not there at the same time, like he was looking into a vapor with fluid edges. There seemed to be an inner glow, her complexion illuminated from within, an aura about her, signaling an unworldliness. Once he was able to put aside his initial impression, he was able to bring more focus, as though he was adjusting a camera lens, to her appearance. Her long, black hair framed an oval face with a translucent porcelain complexion and a barely perceptible scar on her cheek. She wore a white blouse and black pants. When she sat, he noticed red ballet slippers.

He recalled an all-female mime troupe he had once seen in the Golden Gate Park Panhandle who captured its audience's imagination by juggling invisible objects. They performed one routine where a beauty, who looked like the woman sitting before him, suffered a cut to her cheek from invisible knives. The woman dramatically wiped away blood with a flourish and continued to juggle. At the time, he thought it an amateurish magic act. However, as the show continued, there was one trick he could never figure out. The entire troupe of six mimes stood in a circle miming the juggling of each other. It was a dance of sorts, each woman performing jetes across the circle's diameter and pretending to be caught and thrown back to another mime. What began as six mimes leaping, being caught and flung back, mysteriously became five. The mime wearing red ballet slippers vanished into thin air. When the troupe took their bows, the vanishing mime was nowhere to be seen, and he noticed that the remaining five mimes all wore pink ballet slippers.

"What can I do for you?" I asked.

"It's about a man I met." She spoke with a soft, clearly enunciated voice. One that would work well on radio. One that seemed fitting for a mime.

"First thing first, I'm Marvin. And you are?"

"My name does not matter. My story is all that matters."

Marvin looked into her jade green eyes noticing tiny specks of gold, which added depth and allure. She had a story to tell and he was a willing listener. What does her story have to do with his work as a talent agent? Usually, when potential clients come to him, they bring resumes and hints of more than what they represent.

"But you do have a name?" he asked again.

"My name is whatever you need it to be."

She began by telling Marvin she believed she was the protagonist of another's invented story. She added her sentiency was a product of a writer with the power to create authentic reality in a virtual world. What could that possible mean, real objects in an unreal setting? The first time she doubted her own existence was after a one-night stand. She and a stranger met at a coffee shop, drank espressos, and slept together. She told how the entire encounter lacked emotion and a meaningful connection. It was if they were going through someone else's mechanistic maneuvers. They never learned each other's names and parted with no expectation of meeting again.

"What sort of woman would I be if that were real? The experience could only be the fantasy of a lonely man, a very sad man who dreams of sexual encounters with mimes and jugglers."

"What does this have to do with me?" asked Marvin.

"Your grandparents were jugglers and you are a mime. You and your family have a history of trickery and subterfuge. According to the history that I believe has been written for me, my parents were jugglers and Earl and Louise Liebowitz were also my grandparents. We could be distant cousins. We could also be the lovers in that one-night stand."

Not all bombshells are created equal. Marvin had no knowledge or clear memory of this woman. Was this his Ancestry DNA test coming back to haunt him? He had heard of friend's relatives discovering new additions to their family trees after submitting a spit of saliva to any number of genealogy search services. He had submitted his out of curiosity. This might be an example of curiosity stunning Marvin and his alter ego Monsieur Mime. Perhaps, this was all a ruse, a juggler's magic trick, some sort of a scam with a few relevant details. After all, the definition of juggler was varied. It wasn't always about tossing about physical objects. It might also mean organizing information to give a certain impression.

"If you are who you say you are, how do I know if what is happening right now is real?"

"Because reality is what we make of it," she replied. "Juggling, miming, they're part of our shared history, real or not. I've once found myself as part of a female troupe who juggled invisible objects. I was made invisible. I was transported to a place called The Sea Ranch."

Marvin swallowed hard when she mentioned The Sea Ranch. "Wait a second. There's something I just remembered," said Marvin.

On more than one occasion, he performed his Monsieur Mime act at the White Barn Playhouse, a fully renovated structure where The Sea Ranch Thespians produce plays free to the public. Marvin had several clients who owned second homes at The Sea Ranch and he performed his act as a favor. It was one of the few times he received a standing ovation. Free performances seem to bring out the best in audiences.

After one of those freebies, he met the author of a series of young adult books about a juggling troupe. The writer seemed to be aware of Marvin's own family history and connection to mimes and jugglers, which caught Marvin a bit off guard. He dismissed it as his clients sharing his background with The Sea Ranch residents. The writer invited Marvin to his home for dinner. They spent a very pleasant evening sipping Knob Creek rye, having a tasty dinner of pasta a la Bolognese, a crisp green salad, and a fine bottle of zinfandel from the Dry Creek terroir, all prepared by his host.

The writer excitedly told Marvin that he had been experimenting with writing stories with the effect of suspending time and place, creating new dimensions, altered reality, something where nothing before existed. Marvin dismissed the writer as an eccentric with a loose grasp of his own reality. They spent the remainder of the evening with the writer expounding on his theories of "thought transference," the ability of an author to write stories that come alive in another dimension, a kind of parallel universe.

"This isn't about time travel or walking through folds in the universe. It is about a story becoming reality in our time and place, not another's. It's about new definitions of reality that only a writer can create."

Marvin continued listening with ever-increasing thoughts that he was in the presence of a raving lunatic. Or was he in the present? He bid the writer goodnight without exchanging contact information or suggesting they might meet again. As he drove back to the lodge where his clients had arranged for him to stay, he wondered if the experience he just had was worth any more thought. He resolved to put it aside.

Could the absolutely gorgeous woman sitting before him, telling a fantastical tale, have come from an author's mind? Was he born from the same writer's imagination? She told him that her one-night stand was with a man not unlike himself, lanky with an expressive mime's body. He had no recollection of such a night but thought a skilled writer would be good at penning words, as well as erasing them if need be.

Revealing shared grandparents, travels to Sea Ranch, a one-night stand with an unknown man similar in appearance to himself were unsettling. The next revelation also shocked him.

"I've seen you before," she said. "I was performing in the Golden Gate Park Panhandle with an all-female troupe of juggling mimes, jugglers of invisible objects."

Marvin felt a tingling at the base of his skull, his eyes widened, he stared more deeply into her jade green eyes with gold specks that appeared to be twinkling more rapidly. "Go on," he said.

"I was the only one wearing red slippers and disappeared during the human juggling routine. You remember?"

"I do."

"I mean I really disappeared. I wasn't able to take a final bow. I wasn't there anymore."

"Where were you?"

"I think I was knocking on a writer's door at Sea Ranch. It's a faint memory, like a few threads of a blanket that does not provide warmth; rather a covering that causes chills."

Marvin gasped. Perspiration was beginning to bead on his forehead. He felt a slight tremor in his left hand, which was a bad sign for a lower-level mime reliant on total control of his body.

"If we are related through common grandparents, then you must have a name," said Marvin with all the logical calmness he could fathom.

"Apparently, I am a conjuring with little background, few details, and only someone else's story to tell. I am whatever thoughts are given to me."

Marvin told her about his evening with a writer at The Sea Ranch. The more he shared, the brighter her gold specks glowed. The edges of her profile become more defined, less fuzzy, distinct from her aura. Her inner glow dimmed and her face morphed from perfectly smooth and unflawed, lest the slight scar on her cheek, and showed natural pores, normal imperfections...a few tiny birthmarks, translucent hairs above her upper lip.

"How do I know we are not his made-up narrative?" Marvin asked.

"We don't. But I'm feeling this sharing is causing a change in me, which I haven't felt before. I'm feeling more like a relevant being. I'm feeling like I'm more in the here and now. Maybe there's something we can do."

Marvin recalled a conversation he had with his grandparents toward the end of their lives. Marvin asked them how the end of life was different from other times. Did they feel old? How were they able to stay in love for so long? What was it like when they couldn't juggle anymore? Did they feel loss? Did they still look forward with optimism and how did they deal with any regrets they might still have? It was his grandmother's response to his last question that had the most impact on his behavior. It was the reason he did not collect things.

So many of his acquaintances used their collected pictures, souvenirs, art, stamp, matchbook, baseball card collections…tangible objects… as nostalgic mementos. They lived their lives through their possessions. When Marvin asked his grandparents about what things were most memorable in their lives, thinking it would be something he might want to remember them by when they passed, his grandmother said, "Nostalgia is not about stuff, it's about the stories we've lived and tell. Our lives are our stories, not about our possessions. Our stories are all that we have when we leave this dimension."

The power of story. That was the most important lesson Marvin learned from his grandparents. Stories begin at birth, grow over a lifetime, and continue to be told after physical life has ceased. Legacy and story are one.

Marvin took hold of the woman's hands, which felt as real as any hands he had ever held. He told her it made no difference whose story they were in. What mattered was that they were now in the same story and had an awareness that couldn't be taken away. He asked if she would take a ride with him.

Three hours later, they were at The Sea Ranch walking up the path to the writer's home Marvin had once been invited to. They approached the door hand-in-hand, not noticing the neighbor next door watching from his picture window. Before knocking, Marvin asked the woman, "Who are you?"

She replied, "You know who I am."

They smiled at each other and knocked.

Part V
Beyond Unknown

There are times when names don't matter. Those fleeting instances when you pass someone on the street and both take notice with a nod and a half smile, while walking on wondering who that was. It may have been a famous movie star or television personality, but you just can't place their identity. You wish for celebrity but more often it's an ordinary person. Was the nod and smile recognition or simply politeness? Did you have a history? Do you know someone who knows someone who might help make the connection? Those micro moment encounters never make any difference, yet they eat away at your memory. Later, there might be an ah ha moment and you'll recall them at a festive time, a friend's birthday party or business gathering. Or maybe a somber occasion, a funeral or at a favorite candidate's concession speech.

Tik got his name as a toddler when one of the other children in his playgroup couldn't say Rick. The mothers thought it was cute and Tik stuck. The spelling was his father's choice, who thought tick would be confused with tick-tock. Little did they know at the time that Tik Tok would become a social media sensation, which Tik's publisher took full advantage of.

A year had passed since Tik had been at his home in The Sea Ranch. The rights to his latest book, a New York Time's best seller, had been purchased by a film production company. It was the twelfth book in a series about a juggling troupe. Inspired by watching the Flying Karamazov Brothers busking in Golden Gate Park, Tik originally intended the stories for an adolescent audience. He was encouraged to expand his audience and his recent books were well received by adults craving stories with sketchy meanings, double entendres, jugglers and an occasional super hero. It was the idea of the super hero Omniman, an androgynous humanoid with an array of super powers, which caught the attention of several movie studios.

He spent a year away from the quiet culture of The Sea Ranch with screenwriters assisting with the movie adaptation. The money was more than he could ever imagine and he was provided living accommodations in Southern California while working on the project. His companion and best friend Beatrice, a black standard poodle, was always at his side. Tik and Beatrice became a celebrity Hollywood twosome, a frequent item in "Variety." It was, "Mr. Tik and Lovely Beatrice, what can we do for you" by all the waitpersons at fancy-reservation-only restaurants. Passersby who recognized Tik when he was walking Beatrice…hardly ever when he was out alone, would ask, "How is your statuesque companion your inspiration?" Tik was dumbfounded by the attention Beatrice received because of only a few references made in his book series. He thought putting his Pilot fountain pen to paper carried far too much influence. He found the notoriety imposing and soon figured ways to keep himself and Beatrice out of the public's eye. Tik became a recluse in the pricey rental house and lived like the solitary sort he was at The Sea Ranch. Food and other provisions were delivered via the servant's entrance, although no maids, butlers, valets, or other help were employed. Every Wednesday, a team of gardeners tended the front and back gardens. It was the only day Tik did not practice juggling on the patio surrounding a kidney-shaped pool.

He had become a celebrity who learned to nod and smile without sincerity. Regardless of his unremarkable appearance, he attracted followers. How could it be that a tall man with poor posture, untamed reddish-brown hair graying at the temples, ever have followers in Hollywood? After his year among the glitterati, he realized he was nothing more than a pricey hood ornament on an expensive foreign import. The import drew attention; the hood ornament got polished from time to time.

The hired screenwriters assigned to assist him with the adaptation were good listeners but better literary assassins. Whatever he wrote was immediately reimagined regardless of his objections. His story became their story. His characters morphed into stock cinematic images. And his theme of kindness triumphs evil was buried in cinematic flashes of misogynistic violence. Everything he wanted to promote through Omniman, gentleness and kindness, was corrupted. Omniman's feminine attributes were neglected and he was turned into a brutal he-man who used force and caustic sarcasm to fight anti-heroes. Tik felt he was on the verge of becoming a writer trapped in another's story. He quietly resisted hypocrisy by asserting the studio's staff writers had things well under control and suggested he'd rather be considered a ghost screenwriter without any necessary public credit for his contributions. The producers agreed, thanked him for his "revolutionary stories" and bid him farewell.

Tik managed to thank the movie's producers for the privileged life of a year in Hollywood, without any hint of false gratuitousness. Privilege, he thought, was something that ought to be earned, not bestowed. His growing discomfort from a year of extravagant living and the feeling that he had not significantly contributed to a screenplay resembling his original work made it easy to leave. Having a bulging bank account made it even easier.

He packed his personal belongings into two duffle bags, his laptop, pens, notebooks, and Roget's thesaurus in a worn leather `rucksack, and the one souvenir given to him by his literary agent after signing the hefty contract for his book *The Juggler Within Us.* It was a bobble-headed Oscar statuette with its base inscribed, "Winners can't be choosers." His agent's sense of humor was often on the mark and always trite. He drove north in his year-old, hybrid Lexus SUV. He missed his green Morgan roadster, safely garaged and left under the watchful eye of a house sitter in The Sea Ranch but felt it impractical and uncomfortable for a long road trip. He intended to sell the Lexus once he arrived home and got back to normal routines.

He decided to take a leisurely trip. He never liked driving more than a few hours and preferred to stay off busy highways as much as possible. He texted his house sitter informing her that he'd be back at The Sea Ranch in about a week. She replied, "The house will be ready and your friend looks forward to seeing you."

Miranda grew up in Gualala, the little town adjacent to The Sea Ranch, and lived on the kindness of locals, odd jobs, and parents who kept her bedroom available and meals whenever she didn't have other options. She was twenty, with blond hair that sparkled, skin that tanned but never burned, and walked with the delicacy of a fawn. She graduated in the middle rank of her high school class, preferred reading library books over electronic media, used her iPhone for texting, talking, never surfing or searching, and planned to attend community college when the mood was right. She thought of herself as a free spirit and akin to tie-dyed 1960's hippies, the Beatles and lava lamp culture. When she met the writer of juggler stories at the Four-Eyed Frog Bookstore author event, she became a fan, read all of his books, and made herself available for house sitting whenever he traveled.

"What friend?" he texted back. Miranda didn't reply, which wasn't that unusual. Tik had a number of friends who often dropped by without invitation.

Most of Tik's friends were more like acquaintances he had briefly met at author appearances when he would engage in short conversation while signing a book. Some of those conversations led to coffee or a drink at the lodge and an exchange of contact information. Tik's trust in the goodness of others never backfired. His literary agent often chastised Tik for making himself too available.

"The world is becoming weirder and weirder. You need to be careful. Stop giving out your phone number and street address. There are lots of folks out there who are more like your neighbor The Snoop than you'd care to meet. Vulnerability in healthy relationships is a good thing, not with everyone." Tik's agent dispensed excellent literary guidance along with a habit of abundant amateur psychological advice.

Tik had a longstanding issue with his immediate neighbor, dubbed The Snoop, who appeared to always have binoculars at hand, often pointed in Tik's direction. The fact that he had an aggressive miniature poodle didn't help matters. When walking Beatrice along the bluffs, he did whatever he could to avoid that scruffy, mischief-making substandard dog, sometimes even turning around with a call to his meddlesome neighbor that he had forgotten something back at his house.

Tik couldn't think of any others with whom he had issues. He made many new acquaintances while practicing juggling out in front of his home, while Beatrice was curled on her mat watching attentively and often retrieving a dropped ball, apple, tenpin, or other misplayed item. Strangers would stop and ask about his juggling efforts. Beatrice, an excellent judge of human character, would let Tik know if the stranger was worth knowing with her body language and a wagging or non-wagging tail. Wagging was good; a still tail not so much.

The California coast is a lesson in wealth and privacy. Even though Tik lived in a community of the privileged, he was constantly struck by the numbers of people who could afford the luxury of a home bordering the Pacific with the ever-present risk of loss from heavy surf and collapsing hillsides due to fierce storms or the now frequent threat of fire caused by climate change. Regardless of those perils, the wealthy clung to a lifestyle characterized by anonymity and the casualness of costly fashion imitative of common folk in their designer denims, spandex body suits, and overpriced T-shirts. Tik did not own anything custom-made. The Sea Ranch home was comparatively modest. His only luxury the Morgan Roadster, which he had fully restored after purchasing from the estate of a famous juggler. The only condition of sale being that he never reveal the juggler's identity.

He had just passed Big Sur and was heading toward Carmel when his cell phone played Santana's "Evil Ways." It was Miranda calling. Miranda never called, she only texted. Tik pulled to the side of the road and answered.

"What's up? You never call."

"I know, but this woman just showed up and was asking about you. She said it was important. Before she left, I asked for her name and she said you'd know it made no difference. It freaked me out, Tik."

"How so?"

"I mean, she feels creepy. What's the word: cryptic?"

It had been a year. A year working in La La Land. A year since a woman with long dark hair, a tiny scar on her cheek, who walked with the easy grace of gentle Pacific tides, had appeared unannounced at his door, made dinner, spent the night in conversation and left without giving her name. Tik was never sure if the experience was real. There was a dreamlike quality, as though he was living in one of his own stories.

Yet, a few weeks later, she reappeared with Marvin, a mime he had met at a local performance and invited over to his house for dinner. Marvin's story unfolded like a tale Tik had already written. A juggler's story with too many similarities, as well as unexplainable instances.

It was the beginning of dusk when Tik opened his door to Marvin, standing there with the tall woman with jade green eyes and announced, "I've returned with this woman and we have a story to share."

As was his norm and without hesitation, Tik invited them in where they sat in his living room before a large picture window framing the ocean, a sea that seemed to be leaning away from the coastline when it normally leaned in. Tik listened while Marvin and the woman told how they had discovered familial connections between them. Their shared history of mimes and jugglers, the possibility that they were related. The possibility that they were created as the result of one of Tik's stories, and the uncertainty over their own reality.

The woman bore a strong resemblance to a character in one of Tik's stories but Marvin did not. The unknown woman in his short story was a juggler who vanished as part of an act where the invisible objects were tossed about by mimes. Tik had met Marvin in person. He was not an invented character. At least, Tik didn't think he was. But Marvin was a mime. The more he listened to their story, the more he fixated on the ocean. Sometimes it appeared to lean in, sometimes out. Was the Pacific folding time? Creating gaps in reality? Opening a space for conjured events? The woman passionately believed she was a conjuring. She said she felt like a mist risen from the sea and shaped into a human form.

Tik listened, said it must all be coincidence, thanked them for sharing, and ended the evening with the suggestion they might continue the conversation at a later date. Tik found their meeting to be a source of more stories and he spent hours writing story starters in his journal before retiring for the night.

Tik asked Miranda, "What do you mean by 'cryptic'?

"I'm not sure. She seemed to be there and not at the same time. An enigma. She is beautiful, yet transparent. It's hard to explain. I suppose if I believed in ghosts, she might be the first one I've ever met. Do you know her, Tik?"

"I know of her," said Tik. "I don't really know her. Did she say why it was important?"

"Something about myth and identity. She said you'd understand."

"Did she leave any contact information? By any chance, did she mention Marvin?"

"No. She asked when you'd be back and said she'd see you then."

"I wouldn't worry. I'll be home in a couple of days. I'll text you after I cross the Golden Gate Bridge."

The first stop Tik made when he reached San Francisco was the

Panhandle in Golden Gate Park. It was the spot where he first became enamored of jugglers and the worn lawn was like an old friend. Jugglers and mimes inspired his book series and raised questions he had never considered. How might imagination become reality? When did a story become more than the written words? How did the fiction of myths, superstitions and religions become fact?

Every Saturday he found himself seated on an old plaid blanket watching an eclectic group of entertainers, mostly jugglers and mimes with an occasional musician, putting on shows where most of the admirers showed their appreciation by dropping coins and small bills into hats placed about the edges of a defined stage space. It was a group of miming jugglers who gave him the most pause, especially when one woman vanished without acknowledgement or explanation. Tik believed the woman to be the same unknown woman who spent a night with him at The Sea Ranch and returned sometime later with Marvin.

It was unusually cold and the fog wrapped its moist, chilly grip around Tik as he strolled the now empty Panhandle. It was not a good day for performance; rather, a better day for recollection. He dwelled on the evening he spent with the unknown woman, her mysterious appearance, knowledge of his kitchen, the meal she made, her easy familiarity, and the purity of the night filled with conversation and nothing more. Yet the conversation was neither intimate nor illuminating. They spoke of literal and figurative meanings, and the power of metaphor. What did they mean? What was existence? Could someone be there and not there at the same time? Did ghosts, phantasms, apparitions exist only in spirit? Might they be in body? The entire night came down to confusion and not knowing. When the woman left just before dawn, walking into a fog very much like the one Tik now found himself in, he dismissed the experience as a whiskey-induced fantasy. He used their imagined or real involvement to craft another story. It all changed when she showed up with Marvin. Now, she had apparently returned for the third time.

While stopping for gas in Sebastopol, he texted Miranda. He decided to take a longer route home and headed to the coast to Bodega Bay, the site of Alfred Hitchcock's filming of "The Birds" and Patrick's, the purveyor of excellent salt water taffy. He looked forward to picking up a mix of licorice, peppermint, and cherry candies. He pulled up a selection of Bela Bartok music on his iPhone, which he found appropriate to the varied coastal landscape, the ocean moods and drove with an alert determination to solve the mystery of the unknown woman. He felt that the Pacific on his left and the rolling terrain on his right held him safely on the winding road.

Miranda was in the front yard juggling four tennis balls as Tik pulled in. Tik had taught Miranda juggling, telling her it was more than entertainment.

"It builds concentration while drawing others into your circle," he said.

"Concentration is enough for me. I'd like my circle to stay empty for the foreseeable future," Miranda replied. "I'm enjoying the solitary at the moment."

Tik opened the back door of the Lexus, letting Beatrice bound out and over to Miranda for a welcoming scratch behind her ear. He thanked Miranda for taking care of his home for such a long time. For the umpteenth time, Miranda told Tik how appreciative she was of having a place of her own for year, being able to read, and even begin to write some stories of her own. She had already moved her belongings back to her parent's house in Gualala and rode off on her electric bike.

Tik noticed The Snoop walking up the bluff and quickly moved inside. Beatrice's low growl confirmed The Snoop's offish behavior. Tik filled a bowl with Beatrice's first meal of the day, poured himself a Knob Creek rye with two ice cubes, and settled into his leather chair. The ocean was calm with gentle swells rolling in from the familiar fog bank on the horizon. A knock at the door and a single bark from Beatrice broke him from his reverie. Tik opened the door and there she was, the tall woman with long, black hair and binoculars hanging from her neck, wearing a loose-fitting, white linen blouse and black pajama-style pants.

"You've returned."

"Yes. My name is Romy and I've returned to complete our story."

Part VI
A Known Woman

Tik was fascinated by what he called occult entertainment. He thought jugglers, mimes, and magicians existed in another dimension, a world of suspended belief. He drew upon their mystery to write his stories. Over time, he believed their lives and his stories had formed a symbiotic relationship; they influenced his creativity and somehow his creativity reciprocated. These seemingly unexplainable phenomena became clearer after he moved to The Sea Ranch. Each evening, he sat in his leather chair, sipping Knob Creek rye whiskey with his standard poodle Beatrice curled at his feet, watching the Pacific. The sea swells were never the same, sometimes appearing to lean into shore and other times away. Sometimes those tilts formed creases in the ocean's surface. Were those creases evidence of time gaps? Places that existed between reality and another undefined dimension? There were frequent bursts of misty sprays from passing whales on the undulating waters. And then there was what Tik described as water being twisted from those creases and rising high into the air. However, unlike the spew from whales, they were gentler and friendlier sprays. He theorized that they were the result of failed attempts by conjurers to wring mermaids out of their watery domain.

When the unknown woman first appeared at his doorstep, entered, made herself at home in his kitchen, cooked one of his favorite meals, and spent the evening in conversation, he dismissed it as a whiskey-induced dream. A dream, despite the physical evidence of a meal shared and a woman well beyond his imagination. Her second appearance with Marvin surprised him. Tik had once invited Marvin, after his local performance as Monsieur Mime, over for a drink, a pasta Bolognese dinner like the one Romy had prepared, and conversation. It was during that second drop-in visit with Marvin when they shared a well-conceived story of familial connections, a shared history with occult entertainment, and their assertion that Tik had made them come to life through one of his stories. It wasn't till her third appearance, when she finally told Tik her name, that he seriously considered the possibility that his stories might transform the intangible to something tangible. He had once written a story of a mermaid transformed. Might Romy be that character?

Yet, Tik could not reconcile how a mermaid could become human, later a juggler in a mime troupe, disappear into thin air, and visit him on three separate occasions. For what purpose? Tik had written each of those scenarios as individual phenomena but never connected them. He thought of his stories as pleasant enough little tales without violence or salaciousness, and purely for the sort of entertainment one found while people watching on a busy streetcorner.

Again, she stood at his doorstep with the comfort of a woman unafraid of any situation she might confront. A light fog framed her, yet she wore the same clothes as the first time she had stood at Tik's doorstep: a loose fitting, white linen blouse and black pajama-style pants. Tik thought she must be immune to The Sea Ranch's usual chill. Her jade green eyes sparkled with a warm intensity and the slight scar on her cheek from juggling knives, confirmed a history which Tik remembered from his days watching jugglers in Golden Gate Park. Like the first time he met her, Tik tried to notice an aura, a shimmer about her, but didn't. "My name is Romy. I have returned to you with the history you have invented. The history you need to know."

It dawned on Tik that even her name Romy must hold special significance. Where did the name come from? It had to be more than Tik's imagination. Names carried meanings. They didn't pop into a writer's mind out of thin air. Or did they? It couldn't be a coincidence that the Latin meaning of Romy was 'dew of the sea.' Tik thought Romy, a beautiful, dark-haired, mysterious woman, must have emerged from the Pacific just outside Tik's oceanfront home, from one of those ocean creases.

Tik replied, "Then I must know how this story ends."

"I'm not sure you do."

"Please, come inside."

"First, I'll make a meal. You have shrimp in the fridge, right?"

"How did you know?"

"It's in our story."

Romy instructed Tik to pour himself a Knob Creek and relax in his leather chair. Beatrice looked at Romy knowing an old friend had returned and then went and curled before the picture window with the day's setting sun casting light on her curly-haired black body. Tik heard the sounds of pots and pans, water poured into a large pasta pot, the tick of the gas burner lighting, and the smell of lemon zest and juice. He knew Romy was making a lemon shrimp fettuccine dish, another one of his favorite meals.

He watched the Pacific, which seemed to be rocking back and forth, not tilting in or out as it usually did. The sea appeared to be having difficulty making up its mind. Before long, Romy summoned him to the table, asking him to select, uncork and pour a Sauvignon Blanc from his wine fridge. She served him the pasta and a small arugula salad and they ate in silence for a few minutes before she spoke.

"I know you believe I came from the sea, like some sort of transformed mermaid, but that would be a myth begetting a myth. Your imagination created a world over which you have been losing control. To get to the truth of who I am and, more importantly, who you are, you'll need to ask me the right questions."

"Is there a truth? asked Tik.

"That depends on the storyteller. But that's a good first question."

Tik took a bite of pasta, then a shrimp, and thought it the best pasta dish since the first time he encountered Romy. That meal of pasta Bolognese was the flipside of the lemony delight he was now enjoying. Could it be that he and Romy were experiencing inverted stories? Was this some kind of odd symmetry in their lives? An enigmatic entwinement?

"What do you mean, it depends on the storyteller?"

Romy smiled, maintained a steady look at Tik, twirled a strand of fettucine with her fork, and said, "We're both inventions of each other's stories."

Tik noticed the light had returned, the aura, that backlit Romy's silhouette. It was a soft glow, which Tik took as a truth-telling sign. The room felt oddly warm and still. A beam of sunset-filtered light filled the room as though their conversation was in a spotlight.

"What are you saying?"

"You tell stories which have given rise to your own being, sense of self, meaning in a meaningless world. I am here because you need me, just like you need Beatrice, Miranda, Marvin, and even The Snoop next door. You need every character in your life as much as you must walk the bluffs several times a day, and stare at the ocean, the birthplace of your imagination. Your life is your creative imagination. It's no different from mine. Your imagination is your truth. That's no different than mine."

"You're saying I only exist, have purpose, understand meaning because I imagine it. And likewise, you exist only because of your imagination."

"Yes, we are present because of our thoughts and dreams. That is our reality."

Tik took another bite of shrimp. He savored the hint of lemon. It was one of his favorite flavors. For him, lemon meant awakening, an acidic freshness that woke his senses. He looked at Romy, a dew of the sea, and wondered if his own name carried any significant meaning. Was Tik something other than other children's inability to pronounce his given name, Rick.

"It means 'captivating beauty,'" said Romy.

"How did you know what I was thinking."

"You need to understand we're now writing our story together."

"But I don't know what you are thinking."

"You haven't written that part, yet."

Their dialogue ceased. They continued eating in silence. Romy's aura glowed brighter. Tik felt an internal warmth, new to him, and Beatrice seemed to sense a change in the room. She stood and rubbed her muzzle against Tik's leg. Tik scratched behind her ear and told her she was a special dog. They finished their meal, poured second glasses of wine, and sat on the sofa together. The sea had calmed and a sunset was cast across the horizon like an orange bridal veil, all lacy and glittery.

"It's a perfect time for a sea kayak ride."

"I don't have a kayak and it's too late," said Tik.

"I have one at Shell Beach and the full moon will keep the sea light enough. This is all part of our story."

Although the earlier fog had receded to the horizon, there remained a coolness in the air and Tik put on a zippered sweater. Romy had no sweater or coat and stepped confidently ahead as they walked the bluff toward Shell Beach. Beatrice followed dutifully behind, her tail up and her nose sniffing the trail's edge, the path slightly damp from the earlier fog, a full moon lighting the placid ocean, and a lingering sunset set a tranquil, thoughtful mood.

Romy's tandem ocean kayak rested on the beach, reminding Tik of the Harbor seals who lolled on the shoreline just north of Shell beach. Tik looked at the kayak with some trepidation, for he had never tried kayaking.

"It's a bit like juggling," said Romy. "It's all a matter of balance and keeping your eye out front. I'll sit in the back and do most of the work. You'll sit up front and Beatrice can stand or lay down in the bow. We won't need to go far before you fully understand our story."

The Pacific's water was barely lapping onto the shoreline. Small curls of foamy water sliding ashore. Romy pushed the kayak to the water's edge, told Tik and Beatrice to get in, resumed pushing the kayak till it floated free, and then climbed aboard. She used the two-piece paddle to propel them towards the full moon. Beatrice stood, tail wagging like a metronome, its rhythm reminding Tik of a sonata which he couldn't name.

"We're almost there."

Tik felt hypnotized by the sea's gentle swells and the sunset's disappearance when Romy announced that they had arrived. The moonlit ocean widened as a crease formed.

Jugglers were casually tossing a variety of objects back and forth while Tik, Romy, and Beatrice, reclined on a blanket in the Golden Gate Park Panhandle. The memory of an exceptionally fine pasta meal and a sea kayak ride forming a new story.

Quacker Stories

The Quackers

Buzzy and Clara fell in love at the duck pond. Of course, like no other romance, it started with the willowy and vibrative sounds of a saw being played crudely by wannabe professional basketball player Buzzy Mendelsohn. "Somewhere Over the Rainbow" never sounded so awful or so alluring.

Buzzy Mendelsohn is a skinny, almost five-foot six-inch basketball player who once dreamed of being tall. Now he spends much of his time being a gym rat, duck pond visitor and recently an avid saw player. At one time, he was a high school star hoopster with an unbelievable vertical leap, smart ball handling skills and an outstanding outside shot with the ability to get fouled and chalk up a high percentage of free throws. Because of his diminutive size, he was a lightly recruited player by several NCAA Division II colleges. Scouting reports noted his smarts, speed and a skill for creating scoring opportunities for his teammates. His dreams of playing in the NBA remained dreams during the seven years he drifted through several Australian and European teams. He managed to save almost all of what he earned during those years and smartly invested, with lessons learned from his grandfather, his earnings. Those investments now allow him to live comfortably while looking to become a fulltime college coach. He currently coaches at his former high school where his reputation as a player is still very much alive. His coaching responsibilities leave most of his mornings and afternoons with unstructured time. Much of that time he can be found walking through the city park situated across the boulevard from his modest apartment building. When the mood strikes, he totes his thirty-inch Stradivarius musical saw, violin bow and rosin in a custom-made case over to a bench adjacent to the duck pond. He tries to pick a time when there are few others in the park, and he won't be a noisy nuisance. Weekends never work. Thursdays before or after the lunch hour seem best.

When Buzzy and Clara eventually met, the first thing he noticed was her hair. Clara Roth's wavy red hair worn long and full gives the impression that she is in constant motion. Her green eyes sparkle with optimistic anticipation. She is a confident realtor who dresses casually stylish and speaks with clarity and determination. She favors designer jeans, plain white blouses, and espadrilles. Each day begins with a thirty-minute workout in her home gym and three-mile run, part of which is through the park. She is a go-getter and top performer at the firm where she is happy to be an associate and has no ambition to advance as a broker/owner. Even in slow market times, she makes a very good living. At twenty-eight, she has accumulated a sizable number of investment properties and is known as a property owner who keeps her rents fair and her holdings in impeccable condition. Clara loves entertaining friends by playing songs with a comb and tissue paper. When asked why she doesn't simply use a kazoo, she responds by saying a kazoo is problem-free while a comb and tissue paper is an art form. It was her quirky choice of musical instruments that eventually endeared her to Buzzy, just as Buzzy's inharmonious saw had attracted him to her.

One Thursday morning, Buzzy sat on the bench by the duck pond, the handle of his saw clutched between his thighs, his left hand bending the saw and his right gliding the violin bow across the saw's edge. He was working on "While My Guitar Gently Weeps" when a gray-haired woman wearing a large, feathered yellow hat and billowing purple muumuu approached carrying a zither. She sat with perfect posture on the bench beside Buzzy's and asked if she might join in. As Buzzy labored with finding the correct notes, the older woman plucked and strummed the Beatles' classic tune effortlessly. Even the few ducks paddling about the pond seemed to be aware that the music had improved. Her expertise began to influence Buzzy and before long they managed an accurate and workable version. Buzzy's saw was never in such good stead. Buzzy asked the woman if she frequented the park and she said usually on Tuesdays, but she felt that today was a happy accident.

"If you are usually here on Thursday mornings, I'll try to drop by. I'm retired and have a pretty flexible schedule. Actually, I don't really have a schedule. My husband is an avid golfer, my kids live their own lives, and I have my zither. My name is Betty."

For several weeks, they met and developed a short repertoire of duets. From time to time, some of the passersby would stop and listen. Buzzy and Betty quickly developed as an offbeat musical duo with a sturdy friendship. Betty was more than twice Buzzy's age, and it would have been easy for her to assume a motherly relationship with him. However, it was more of a buddy-to-buddy connection. Betty was quick with crude humor. "I hope you're not as limp as your saw when it counts. Hold that bow like your girlfriend and caress her with a gentleness that makes her swoon." Buzzy often blushed and, when he revealed that he didn't currently have a girlfriend, Betty said that needed to be fixed. "A nice young man like you needs a woman in your life. No wonder you are so heavy-handed on that saw."

One day Betty mentioned that she had some friends who enjoyed playing instruments not generally considered mainstream and asked if it would be okay to invite them to play with them. Buzzy, who was gaining confidence with the saw, didn't see a problem and looked forward to playing with others. And so, the duet grew to a septet with the addition of a slide whistle, washboard, Jew's harp, triangle, and castanets. The slide whistle added an ethereal element with its wispy background tones.

The washboard player eschewed metal thimbles for Lee's Press-on Nails saying it gave a softer percussive sound that wasn't as forward as metal on metal. The Jew's harpist offered a haunting, distant and persuasive sound when used judiciously. And the triangle and castanets provided subtle punctuation when called upon.

By default, Buzzy and Betty shared leadership. Buzzy's musical talent was intuitive while Betty's was learned. She was thought to be the only one in the group who could read music, although that never mattered. It was a play-by-ear that relied on musical memory type of group. If someone could hum the tune, they could play it. They enjoyed working things out. Anyone might suggest a song to play and Buzzy and Betty would deliberate for a few moments before deciding if they would give it a try. Buzzy had a talent for being able to listen to the whole group and simultaneously the individual instruments while they played. He was able to make suggestions about the arrangement and how their playing could be tweaked to make a combination of instruments, which in theory didn't belong together, sound like they did. Other than Betty and the Jew's harp player, Buzzy didn't refer to each player by name; rather he simply referred to them by instrument. "That sounds perfect washboard. A little softer slide whistle." The Jew's harp player's name was Zelda Bronstein and Buzzy, being a Jew, felt he ought to call her by her given name and not her instrument. "Nice job, Jew's harp" didn't sound quite right or politically correct.

Zelda was the first to suggest that they give their group a name. Betty enthusiastically agreed and triangle said, "How about the Duck Pond Band?" Washboard added, "I'm thinking the Unconventional Duck Pond Noisemakers, since "'band' might be too much of a stretch." More suggestions were thrown out and they finally agreed to call themselves the Weird Duck Pond Ensemble Gone Quackers. Castanets, who came up with the name, preferred puns and slide whistle thought they were "just plain weird." They ended up referring to themselves as the Quackers and even thought about adding a duck call to the group but decided it would be an inflexible instrument and too representative of a culture none of them held in much esteem.

Betty proposed they expand by one more player to make them an octet. "It's a nice even number and I know a woman who might be an interesting addition. She happens to own my apartment building and I've heard she likes to play the comb. She's busy with a successful real estate career but, like me, seems to have very flexible time." No one objected and on the following Thursday Betty introduced Clara to the group.

Clara strolled up to the Quackers carrying a longer-than-usual comb wrapped in trailing pink tissue paper. Her red hair looked like an explosion organized by a gifted stylist. Her smile full of welcome and her lithe stature full of energy. Buzzy was put off by the brashness of the pink tissue paper but instantly attracted to her natural red hair. And then Betty asked Clara to give the group a sample of her playing. Clara skillfully played a lively rendition of "Oh, Susannah."

"Well, it's not really in our wheelhouse, but you certainly have potential," said Buzzy. "How about trying The Doors' "Light My Fire."

"Not a problem," replied Clara. Her enthusiastic version impressed the Quackers, and Zelda immediately invited her to join the group. Buzzy and Betty agreed and now the Quackers were an octet.

Clara faithfully showed up every Thursday morning regardless of her busy schedule with her red hair alive and her energy intoxicating. She amused the Quackers with her comb wrapped in a variety of tissue paper color choices, which she rotated from week to week: pink, blue, yellow, red, and green. She used a full sheet of tissue paper, which fluttered softly in the breeze like a victory flag. Clara was the only fully employed member of the Quackers and was always dressed for work while the rest of the group looked a bit like a ragtag collection of idiosyncrasies.

The Quackers were developing something of an oddball reputation around the duck pond. Regulars and irregulars alike were showing up in increasing numbers. Observers kept offering donations, but the octet kept themselves free of gratuities. Zelda always explained that they were there for fun and amusement only. It was after six months of building a broad repertoire of rock, country-western, and folk music when Clara spoke up for the first time and recommended that they try something classical. "Let's try "Clare de Lune." I think it was made for the saw." Buzzy stared open-mouthed. Betty began directing supporting roles for the other players by humming their parts before Clara interrupted with an abbreviated comb version.

Their first date was shortly after "Clare de Lune." They sat across from one another in a forgotten coffee shop. The type where the owners were going for the retro look but ended up with a schlocky version of imagined yesteryear: black and white linoleum floor tiles, Formica-topped tables and red Naugahyde chairs. They were served by women dressed like Alice and Flo from Mel's Diner who tried acting gruff with hearts of gold and insisted on being called waitresses. They ordered root beer floats and a plate of fries. "We ought to pretend we're teenagers again," said Clara. "For some reason, I'm feeling a sense of adolescent first date jitters with you."

It was the beginning of a conversation that immediately went deeper than any Buzzy had ever experienced with a date. Once they reviewed their short histories…family, schooling, work, and what they enjoyed doing in their free time…which Buzzy was happy to learn was Clara's regular workout routine…. Clara turned serious and asked, "What has been your biggest regret?"

"That's an odd question?" said Buzzy. "Maybe you should go first. I'm not sure I'm old enough to have big regrets."

"Mine is easy. I regret not having learned to play the piano and continuing with the violin. And now I seem to be stuck with a comb."

Buzzy asked, "You play the violin?"

"I did. It's been almost a year since I put it away."

"You quit?"

"Let's say I'm on a hiatus."

"A hiatus? You plan to go back?"

"I plan to think about it." With that Clara looked down at her hands resting on her lap and appeared to be somewhere in the past. Buzzy noticed a sadness around her half-closed eyes but didn't say anything. After a few moments of appearing to be in a trance, Clara's eyes opened fully with a familiar gleam and she asked again, "What about your regret, Buzzy? You can't use your age as an excuse."

"Well, I can't say it isn't making into the NBA. It was something I dreamed of and worked my butt off to achieve. I'm happy with the effort and know that my talent is as a coach and I'll continue to work toward bigger and better opportunities. No, my regret is not having spent enough time listening and collecting stories from my grandfather."

At the mention of grandfather, Clara leaned in, rested her chin on her right hand and listened to Buzzy's story with increased attention.

Buzzy told how his grandfather Dvorak, named after his father's favorite composer, was a self-made man. He grew up near Coney Island a short, scrawny outcast who quit school at sixteen and ran away from home with fifty dollars in his pocket, a heavy Navy pea jacket to protect him from winter's cold, and a backpack filled a few changes of clothes, a toothbrush and toothpaste (he was always proud of his smile) and a fistful of candy bars. He hitchhiked across country to Portland. His parents and five siblings gave up looking for him after a month and were relieved and disappointed when he finally called four months later to tell him he was fine and finding a new life in Portland.

His thumb and sparkling grin made it easy to secure rides and he met drivers full of kindness and stories to tell as he made his indirect journey to his goal of finding freedom from his overbearing family and meaningless high school, where he excelled in mathematics and class clownish antics. By the time he reached his destination, he had accumulated over three hundred dollars from the strangers who offered him rides, meals, places to stay, and a few dollars to help him along the way. He was struck by the generosity of others and was determined to give back when he could.

When he arrived in Portland, he found a cheap motel and an abandoned grocery cart. One thing he learned from his journey was the value of junk. He met one long haul truck driver who had a collection of items he found in his travels. He marveled at what others either threw away or simply lost. He began collecting found objects, cleaning them up, and in some cases learned how to repair broken items. Some of the most valuable items he found were jewelry and watches. He bargained lessons in watch repair from an independent jeweler who traded expertise for janitorial work. He spent weekends at local flea markets making a good profit from his industriousness. By the time he turned twenty-one and enjoyed his first legal beer at a local pizza joint, he had rented a workbench from the jeweler/mentor he had befriended and had three "employees" who scoured neighborhoods for repairable items. The jeweler frequently asked Dvorak if he would be a full-time employee and offered a good salary and benefits. He explained that he was nearing retirement and would offer the business at a fair price. Dvorak consistently declined and said he preferred the freedom that junk afforded. At twenty-five, he had twelve employees, whom he paid a regular salary and who worked multiple flea markets in and around Portland. He was earning enough to purchase his first home, a small bungalow in Milwaukie on the outskirts of Portland. Finding, repairing and selling five Rolex watches was enough for the down payment. He was also paying taxes and investing in a retirement account. His gift of math taught him about compound interest, and he was sharp enough to know that early investments would pay huge dividends in later life.

Dvorak married Flipside, the free-spirited daughter of hippies, and they had two children, Bruce and Chet, by the time he was thirty. Chet eventually became Buzzy's father.

Clara listened while sipping at her root beer float and using the straw to mix in the vanilla ice cream. Buzzy had spoken non-stop for almost thirty minutes. Clara's soda had gone flat, and the ice cream was nothing more than a creamy wisp. Clara commented that Buzzy seemed to know Dvorak's entire history and asked, again, what was it that he regretted. Buzzy paused, focused his blue eyes to the side seeming to seek out more memories before responding.

"I knew from my grandfather's stories how he turned what his family thought was a wasted life into a successful enterprise and a small empire built on what others threw away. I learned how perseverance and an independent grit might be more important qualities than genius. What I didn't learn was how he felt, how he fell for my grandmother, how he felt when she died suddenly and much too early; what it was like to raise two sons on his own; what he thought about dying when he knew his own end was near. I never learned why he never went to shul and why he insisted that I do and even finish my Bar Mitzvah. I never asked why he faithfully attended my basketball games through high school and college and encouraged me to be a pro even though I never had a realistic chance. I never asked why he smoked smelly cigars and drank cheap whiskey, but never to excess. I never learned why he didn't remarry and why he insisted that I only marry a girl I deeply loved. He would tell me, "Don't accept okay, only say yes to spectacular." I'm not sure what he meant by 'spectacular.' I never learned about his motivation or interior life."

Buzzy finished and Clara felt on the verge of love with an unfamiliar flutter in her stomach. She was beginning to think she had met spectacular.

Then she was asked about her biggest regret. She pushed aside her half-drunk float and the plate of hardly touched fries, reached across the table to took Buzzy's hands into her own and said, "Not continuing to play a real instrument and not yet falling in love."

"I'm serious, Clara. Other than your penchant for playing a comb with loud flowing tissue paper, I don't know you. Really, what is your biggest regret?"

Clara withdrew her hands and sat back. "Buzzy, my last name is Rothstein. I never told you that. I held back a piece of my history because I feared that we might have too much in common."

She told of her great grandparents and their survival from the Holocaust. "They were very old when I knew them, but I'll never be able to erase the memory of seeing faded numbers tattooed on their arms. They protected me from their story and the terror of that time, but I regret not asking. I regret not asking their only child, my grandfather, what he knew before he passed. I regret not asking about their intimate histories. You have a history without feelings; I have feelings without a history."

"And that's your biggest regret?" asked Buzzy. "You have feelings without a history."

"Well, yes, to a certain degree. I also regret not playing my violin anymore. My grandparents gave me that violin years before I ever took a lesson or even considered wanting to play an instrument of any kind. I think it was a way of planting a dream of theirs inside me."

Family legend informed of a distant uncle Isadore who had been a violin protégé and initially taught himself to play on a borrowed half-size violin at age three by listening to his parent's collection of classical records. Between the Great World Wars, Isadore grew up in Berlin, an only child of well-to-do entrepreneurs. His mother played music while she tended to household chores and Isadore, a smiling and contented child, concentrated on using the small violin to mimic the sounds emanating from his parents' record player. The family story tells how Isadore began formal lessons at age five, began playing in the youth symphony at seven and became its concertmaster at nine. He began giving solo recitals at fancy, private engagements in the homes of prominent wealthy Germans and his family was approached by an American music agent who wanted to arrange series of concerts in New York, Boston and Philadelphia. His violin was silenced forever when he and his family were murdered in the Holocaust.

Clara told how she played in her high school orchestra and the local youth symphony. Her parents thought she should major in music when she went off to college. She played in a few chamber groups but was more interested in business and having a career where success is measured in currency. Up until a year ago she continued to play with a few friends but put it aside for no discernable reason. She didn't know if she became bored or simply too busy with other interests. Her violin sits on the top shelf of her bedroom closet, where it's been for the last year.

"Now I've become a musical caricature with a tissue-covered comb."

"A beautiful one at that," added Buzzy.

Clara was a duck pond no-show for two months. The Quackers continued to build musical selections connected by whimsy rather than genre or theme. She and Buzzy met two or three times each week for a walk or a meal. Their conversations becoming deeper and more intimate. When Buzzy asked why she wasn't playing with the group anymore, she said she was giving up the comb for more serious musical pursuits.

"Back to the violin?"

"I'm trying."

"You are trying to resurrect dreams."

"No, I'm trying to honor my regrets rather than being stuck in them."

When Clara eventually returned to the Quackers, she was carrying her violin case. The Quackers were in the middle of playing the theme song "My Heart Will Go On" from the movie "Titanic." Buzzy's saw was in fine form and Betty's zither perfectly underscored the music's melancholy. The other instruments were silent for the duet. Clara stood behind a small audience of appreciative onlookers, mostly regulars with a few amused newbies. Clara's quiet smile and a few tears went unnoticed by all the Quackers except for Zelda who walked over to Clara and whispered, "He's really gotten pretty good. Are you ready to play today?"

Clara replied, "More than you can possibly know."

The audience broke into enthusiastic applause. Buzzy looked up, noticed Clara and waved for her to join them. "It's been a while since our comb player has been here. Please, welcome back Clara." Betty put down her zither and welcomed Clara with a warm hug. Slide whistle and washboard played a quick flourish.

Clara announced that she was happy to return but not as a comb player. She placed her violin case on the bench next to Betty, opened it and tenderly removed a dark grained violin. She tightened the bow strings, played several notes to properly tune her instrument. Addressing the audience, she said, "I love the Quackers, and I love Buzzy. But I'm no longer part of the group. I've chosen a different path or should I say I've decided to return to my real dream. This violin is all that survives from my Uncle Isadore and I want to play a tribute to him."

Clara played the theme from the movie "Schindler's List." While she played, Zelda built a small stone cairn next to the duck pond and Buzzy wept.

Betty Learns to Cope

Family legend has it that the moment Betty Cavanaugh was able to differentiate colors she chose purple. Except for bright yellow hats, which sometimes bordered on being fluorescent, everything she wore was a variation of purple: undergarments to winter coats and lingerie to fluffy terrycloth robes, with the only exception being shoes and other accoutrements such as belts, scarves and jewelry. Betty had a signature style dominated by purple and fanciful yellow hats. Throughout her childhood, adolescence, and much of her adulthood, she was known as the woman who wore purple and played the zither.

She discovered the zither when attending a Lovin' Spoonful concert where John Sebastian happily strummed an autoharp while singing "Do You Believe in Magic." Shortly thereafter, she convinced her piano teacher, who happened to also play a zither in a bluegrass band, to tutor her in the zither. She eventually gave up on the piano (much to her parent's and teacher's dismay) and became what her friends called a "purpled zitherist." With a warm smile and a hug, Betty's kind demeanor, ribald sense of humor and welcoming spirit endeared her to everyone she met. She knew no boundaries when it came offering affection and a helping hand.

Betty and Zelda became close friends while playing with the Quackers, a hybrid musical group featuring Betty playing zither, Buzzy Mendelsohn on musical saw, Zelda on Jew's Harp and a small collection of other off-beat instrumentalists, notably Clara Roth whom Buzzy eventually married. Clara joined the Quackers as a tissue paper and comb player before returning to her beloved violin. The Quackers disbanded shortly after Betty's husband Marcus collapsed from a sudden and massive heart attack while playing golf. Betty became a widow in her mid-60's and Zelda became the shoulder she could comfortably cry on. Zelda insisted that non-religious Betty sit a modified shiva – no covered mirrors, no low stools on which to sit uncomfortably, no torn clothes, no minyan, nothing religious or Jewish - and mourn her husband with the support of family and friends. When the week of quiet solitude and introspection ended, Betty turned to Zelda and asked with sad eyes, "Besides all the tears and sympathy, how am I supposed to really cope?"

Zelda shrugged her shoulders and responded, "We simply cope. Every day we cope."

Betty thought a long time about coping. She and Marcus had what their friends described as a solid marriage. Marcus was a socially conservative financial advisor who fell in love with his "purple queen" in their mid-30's. He was firmly established in his career and Betty owned a small women's boutique selling vintage clothing or what others called "second chance clothing," which was popular with the more artistically inclined who viewed the store as an upscale Goodwill. With advice from friends that, as a single woman with a small business, she should seek long-term financial planning, Betty walked into Marcus's office without an appointment, dressed in a bright, loose-fitting mauve dress and yellow feather-plumed bowler hat. She approached the receptionist and asked to see a feminist who could give good financial advice. The receptionist replied that Marcus Cavanaugh was an independent certified financial advisor and definitely "a feminist at heart." Betty was amused by the sign on the receptionist desk that read, "In charge until further notice."

"Okay, I'll try him out."

"You'll need an appointment," said the receptionist.

"Oh, is he not available right now?"

At that moment, Marcus emerged from his office wearing a summer-weight tan suit, baby blue dress shirt and royal purple tie. He was immediately struck by Betty's perfect posture, eye-catching ensemble and her aura of confidence, which he noticed in few women. He informed his receptionist that he had some time and would be happy to see a new client. Betty's eye was drawn to Marcus's tie, slender physique, dimpled cheeks, a Kirk Douglas chin and easy smile. He showed her into his office and invited her to sit in a leather chair facing his. This was not an I-sit-behind-a-desk-while-you-sit-across-in-a-client-chair power office arrangement. Marcus casually picked up a legal tablet, pulled a pen from his breast pocket and asked how he might be of assistance.

After almost thirty years of marriage, a loving son and daughter, three grandchildren whom she adored, and a life free from financial worry due to sound financial planning, Marcus was gone in an instant.

"We cope?' asked Betty again.

"Yes."

Betty wondered about what that might mean. Was it merely facing difficulty and coming to terms with it? Was it purely an emotional response or did it require physical action? Did it involve interacting with others or an internal story she created for herself? Would she be stuck in the present or could she move forward and learn to leave her sorrow behind? Was grief something that faded as a result of coping with it?

"Zelda, I'm not going to do what I know others have done when they've lost a spouse. I'm not going to do what others expect me to do. I'm not going to dispose of his clothes and personal items. I'm going to let them remain as they are for however long they need to remain. Instead, let's clean out my closet and then go shopping. It's time for a transformation. And then let's go sign up for golf lessons and also that Formula One racing school for beginners. Actually, forget the golf lessons; let's learn to drive a race car."

Betty called her daughter Phoebe to inform her of her plans. Phoebe was the oldest of her two children. She did not inherit her mother's flair for purple; rather, she presented herself like her father: outwardly conservative with a liberal core. She worked as a social worker and shared equal parenting duties with her realtor husband for her two children. When her father died, she took a short bereavement leave wishing to spend more time with her mother. Her mother's call came as a complete surprise.

"Mom, you need to wait a while before doing something crazy. Racing school? You could get hurt and maybe hurt someone else. You can't put yourself and Zelda at risk!"

"First, I appreciate your concern, but I need to get in motion. I'm not just going to sit around the house and grieve. I can mourn while learning to cope. By the way, how is my offspring and the offspring of my offspring? You know I love you very much."

"Now I'm an offspring! What's that supposed to mean."

"Just trying to lighten the moment."

Phoebe stressed that her mother should wait at least a year before doing anything radical. It dawned on Betty that parent/child roles were being reversed. She wasn't surprised. She and Marcus raised strong independent children and hoped they might be there to care for them as they aged. She felt a sense of parental pride as she listened to Phoebe giving her advice.

"Marcus and I didn't talk much about what would happen if one of us died before the other. But, when we did talk about it, he was clear, and so was I, that life needed to go on. I don't think Marcus would just want me to hunker down in a tunnel of sadness. I don't really believe that you or your brother wants that either. I know Zelda doesn't. And I know I don't want that kind of life. I'm going to have some adventures while adventuring is still possible. Shiva, whatever that was, is over."

Betty called Marcus Jr. and arranged to meet him for lunch. "M.J., I have something important to tell you."

"Mom, Phoebe already called. I'm fine with whatever you're going to do. Dad used to say, "You only live once so make sure one and done is more than fun."

Betty laughed knowingly and said, "Your dad did have a way with someone else's words."

Half a year later, wearing her now signature all white outfits, hair clipped short with raspberry highlights and donning only a purple baseball hat, Betty ran her red Mazda Miata into a roadside ditch. Neither she nor Zelda were injured, although Betty felt extreme guilt considering she had passed race driving school with special kudos from the instructor and a warning to not try to be a race car driver on public roads. Betty did show a newfound proclivity for speed. There had already been too many close calls when passing slower cars on two-lane highways and trying to beat every yellow light at city intersections. As a passenger, Zelda had developed the habit of riding with her eyes closed. She was convinced that Betty would eventually kill them both, yet she continued to subject herself to Betty's harrowing rides.

The AAA tow truck pulled the Miata from the ditch and there didn't appear to be much damage. The worst of it being scraped paint on the passenger side, a dented right front fender and broken headlight. The tow truck driver gave Betty and Zelda a ride to a recommended auto repair shop. The initial estimate was lower than expected and Betty was told the car would be ready in less than two weeks. Betty was provided a rental car with the admonition to not exceed the speed limit. Betty's insurance agent had the same words of advice.

On the way home, Betty turned to Zelda and said, "We're alive and I'm continuing to learn to cope."

"Well, if learning to cope is almost killing yourself and me in the process, maybe learning to cope isn't such a great idea."

Fortunately, Betty began to tone down her driving. She traded her repaired Miata for an SUV hybrid and suggested that she and Zelda go on a road trip. "Let's go visit some of the Quackers."

"Betty, when's the last time you played your zither?"

"When the group broke up. I lost motivation. I haven't even thought about it since Marcus died."

"We need to go back to the duck pond and play some music. Then we can go visit Buzzy and Clara."

Returning to the duck pond felt more like trying to return to Marcus rather than the Quackers. Dressed in a white, baggy shift and carrying her zither for the first time in several years, Betty approached with a nervous twitter in her stomach. Her usual confidence waning like one of the shy ducks swimming alone on greenish water. Zelda carried her Jew's Harp with pluck and sure strides. Zelda wasn't known for having her own fashion sense and had taken to also wearing all white when with Betty. They sat together on a familiar bench and Betty began playing the theme from the movie "The Third Man," which, in Betty's opinion, was the greatest zither song ever. It was also Marcus's favorite. Zelda sat quietly holding her Jew's Harp like any best friend would in a moment when being present was all that was necessary.

There were no others at the duck pond while Betty played with all the skill and panache she always had. The music seemed to underscore the mystery captured in the classic film noir cinema. Betty always believed the song was a perfect combination of fanciful movement and intrigue. She plucked and strummed the zither with eyes closed and a gentle swaying from side to side. She was lost in the memory of Marcus, the Quackers, purple clothes with yellow hats and Zelda's support.

Bungee jumping came to Betty in a dream and that felt like a revelation. She woke, Googled locations and organizations, and called

Zelda. "Pack your bag, pack your adult diapers, pack your courage. We're going to New Mexico to jump off a bridge."

The actual jump turned out to be less of a thrill than either Betty or Zelda imagined. With no pun intended, they both wore white jumpsuits, white New Balance tennis shoes, white headbands and gleaming white smiles. They were the first two jumpers off the Gorge Bridge in New Mexico as a dozen twenty and thirty somethings cheered their freefalls. Two more jumps later and they were satisfied and ready to move on to whatever adventure awaited. All the jumpers celebrated with a lavish picnic and cold beers.

A petite woman with spiked magenta-tipped hair in her early twenties asked why two women "my grandma's age" wanted to go bungee jumping. "And you didn't even seem nervous or scared or having second thoughts."

Zelda explained that she was along to support her dear friend and help her cope with the loss of her husband. "I guess you might say we are growing older without becoming old. My friend Betty is finding a way to cope with change by changing."

"My friend Zelda has me figured out," said Betty.

The young woman stared at Betty and Zelda like a lost pet who found a nurturing home. Betty and Zelda represented strength and vulnerability. "What do you do when you're not bungee jumping off bridges?"

"We do pretty much what other women our age do," replied Zelda.

Betty added, "Yes, we stay in touch with family and friends, dote on our grandkids, go shopping, eat out too much and do all the things we want to do now that we have time."

"But you're alone without your partner," said the young woman with a look of concern. "It's so sad."

Betty smiled and reached for the young woman's hand and said,

"It's the nature of coping."

On the drive back to their hotel, Zelda asked, "What's next on your give-me-a-heart-attack list?"

Betty glanced over at Zelda who was leaning against the SUV's side-door window looking like a teenager asking for an assignment. It dawned on Betty that she'd been making all the decisions while Zelda dutifully followed along. She wondered if anyone could ever have a better friend. Marcus insisted on equity. She and Marcus even alternated making vacation choices. They would throw out ideas, which they would discuss at length, before acceding to whoever was the next decider. Usually, Marcus decided upon whatever Betty wanted, so it made little difference whose turn it was. Marcus told their friends that equity was making sure Betty got what she wanted. Betty told the same friends that equity was believing things were equitable. Betty was concerned about the equitable balance between her and her best friend.

"I think it's beyond time for you to get a choice. What would you like to do, Zelda?"

"Well, I want to wear color again. Not just one color but a range of bright, happy colors. And I want to visit Buzzy and Clara."

Buzzy and Clara were a two-day drive away. When Zelda called to ask if she and Betty could visit, they enthusiastically encouraged them to stay with them and for as long as they'd like. Betty and Zelda had not seen Buzzy and Clara since their wedding and subsequent move to the small college town where Buzzy was gaining a reputation as an outstanding college coach and Clara was able to remotely manage her many properties and also play in several string chamber groups.

Zelda was driving the last leg of their trip to Buzzy and Clara's home when Betty turned to Zelda and said, "I think I'm coming to terms with whatever coping is."

"You are."

"Yes. It's not all that complicated. Coping is distance plus time. And we've been taking the time to put some distance between Marcus's death and the now."

"Not very profound," said Zelda.

"Nope. Nothing ever is."

Simple is a State of Mind

Simplicity is often a dream. For some it means cleaning the house, disposing of unused stuff by donating it to the Goodwill, and maintaining a scaled down orderliness. For others it's not merely the external straightening out of tangible belongings but more about creating an inner sanctuary of peace, order and purpose. Karl "Flip Kon" Konstantin was a well-known trombone player among an elite group of jazz afficionados. He was dubbed "Flip" by the band's drummer who noticed that Karl flipped his wrist like a loose hinge when playing upbeat songs. His day job was spent working as a lead school custodian and playing on weekends with a small jazz band at a series of local clubs and coffee houses for tips and quiet recognition. Playing jazz gave him peace and order. Eventually he would discover that a slide whistle would bring him purpose.

It was a foggy March morning the day Flip was born. The doctors and nurses confirmed to his anxious, first-time parents that he was perfectly normal. Flip's parents thought he was too small according to their family histories where everyone…parents and siblings…were very tall. Flip didn't remain small for long. By the time he started pre-school, he was the tallest child and continued to grow taller and taller without an end in sight. He reached his full six-foot six-inch height by the end of eighth grade with sore knees and no desire, no matter how persuasive the coaches could be, to play basketball or any other sport for that matter. He had enough self-awareness to know that he had very little control over his gangly body. He was also uncomfortable with all the stares and not-so-quiet whispers made by some of his classmates. Walking through his high school corridors, his long brown hair bobbing every which way, was an example of motion in multiple directions: arms and elbows, legs and knees appearing to move in opposition to one another. Fortunately, he had fallen in love with the trombone in elementary school and spent all his free time practicing alone in his bedroom and later in junior high school with a small group of like-minded musician friends. He was an average student academically with no college plans but an above-average trombone player with the dream of being a professional musician.

After high school graduation, he secured a job as a substitute janitor, which turned into an assistant janitor then regular janitor and after ten years the head custodian at his former elementary school. Some of his former teachers remembered him as "a likable but unmotivated average student." They were pleased and not surprised when he returned as the school's head custodian. The biggest difference they noted with Flip since his school days was his coordination, neatly barbered appearance and a propensity for whistling jazzy tunes while working. The school's principal frequently commended Flip on his work ethic and attention to detail.

The school children were always aware and entertained by the tall janitor who was constantly whistling. Flip, not yet married, enjoyed the kids who whistled back at him. The older children who had already learned to whistle would even try to join him in whistling along. Flip took the time to help the younger children learn how to whistle. "Pinch your lips into a circle like mine and blow. Blow gently, like you are trying to wake your pet cat or dog by blowing into their faces." Over time, Flip had a regular collection of groupies who would linger in the cafeteria after finishing their lunch and whistle tunes along with Flip while they helped him clean up.

Flip and his bandmates were enjoying a beer after a Saturday night gig. Flip shared how much he enjoyed the children who hung out to whistle with him. "It's a shame they don't offer music lessons at the elementary school anymore. I don't think I'd be playing trombone if I hadn't begun in fifth grade."

The band's drummer suggested, "You ought to get the kids involved in some sort of instrument. Something simple and easy. No need for music lessons; just have fun."

Flip approached the school's principal with the idea of forming a slide whistle and kazoo after-school club. He thought choosing an instrument that didn't require anything other than breath and enthusiasm would be a good introduction to playing music together. "I'm done at 3:00 and there are still plenty of kids hanging around. I'll supply the instruments. It'll be a fun thing to do." The principal agreed and offered to pay for the instruments, but Flip insisted on purchasing them himself. The Fiesta School Slide Whistle and Kazoo Band was an instant success. Every Thursday afternoon, Flip spent an hour demonstrating a tune and then taking his charges on a march around the school grounds making joyful noise. A group of parents were impressed by Flip and his group of what they called "happy strutters." They raised enough money among themselves to purchase T-shirts for the band. One of the parents did some research and learned that a slide whistle also went by the name swanee. The front of the shirt read "Fiesta Swanee & Kazoo Band" and on the back "Joyful Noise."

One crisp November day, a week before Thanksgiving, the aunt of one of the fourth-grade slide whistlers approached and introduced herself.

"I'm Betty. You really have a way of working with these kids. My nephew Aaron can't stop talking about you."

Betty told Flip about The Quackers, a group of off-beat musicians who met each Thursday morning. "If you ever have a Thursday morning off, come on by and play with us. We could use a slide whistle. I play zither with a saw player and, so far, a washboard and Jew's Harp."

Coincidentally, Flip had just been offered a Saturday morning custodial job. The four-hour pay was double time, and he could exchange that morning for any regular weekday. Flip didn't hesitate to accept and looked forward to using his Thursday off day to play with The Quackers in the morning and the Fiesta Slide Whistle and Kazoo Band in the afternoons.

Flip didn't reveal to The Quackers that he played trombone. It was clear from the moment he joined the odd assortment of musicians at the duck pond that Betty was the only other one with any formal musical training. He'd simply show up with slide whistle in hand and stay in the background using his high-pitched instrument to accent or underscore the pieces they played. Sometimes he'd add a vibrato to emphasize a particular flourish but generally kept his sound pure and clean. There was no music to be read, just the encouragement and suggestions from Buzzy, the saw player, and Betty, who strummed and plucked the zither with true expertise.

Buzzy never called Flip by name. It was always, "Slide whistle, nice job accenting that piece. Maybe a little more whoop at the end." Flip smiled, played again with more "whoop" and enjoyed what he began to refer to as the "Zen of the musical moment." He'd tell his jazz band mates about The Quackers and once-in-a-while one would show up to watch the group play. When his drummer came by, he would call out, "Way to go Flip "Slide Whistle" Kon! More slide whistle!" Flip would try to shun any singling out with a wave of his hand but eventually gave up and apologized to The Quackers after they had finished playing. He didn't want attention; it took away from the simple act of playing music different from anything he played on Saturday nights. However, due to the drummer's good-natured calling out, Flip "Slide Whistle" Kon became not only his Quacker name but also how his jazz band referred to him.

One morning after The Quackers had finished a spirited rendition of Queen's "Bohemian Rhapsody," Betty invited Flip to lunch. "I want to talk to you about my nephew Aaron." They sat at a booth at Moshe's Deli where Betty ordered a Greek salad and raspberry lemonade and Flip an egg salad sandwich on marble rye bread and black coffee. Betty told Flip how her nephew had always been a very introverted child.

"At first, his parents and I thought he might have some sort of developmental issue, but doctors told us he was just what they termed a "slower than normal developer" and not to worry. He always lagged behind children his same age. He was the last to learn how to walk. He struggled with reading but did find arithmetic easy. His parents and I were very concerned he might need to be tested again for special education, but then you helped him to discover the slide whistle. It's changed his life."

Betty looked across the table like an older sister proud of her accomplished brother. Flip wasn't sure how to respond and looked back with a Cheshire grin at Betty, who wore a bright yellow bowler hat and a purple scarf over a lavender dress. He took a sip of coffee and cleared his throat before responding, "I think that's one of the nicest things anyone has ever said to me."

"He's become a different child. He talks nonstop about the Fiesta Band. For some reason, he's begun to read more and seems to enjoy it. His teachers have reported that he has made significant strides academically and is now at or above grade level in all his subjects."

"It's just a slide whistle," said Flip.

"It's more than that. I think it's a feeling of belonging, of being noticed, of purpose."

Flip left the deli feeling like an explorer who had just discovered a new land. Betty had caused him to pay a different kind of attention to his own sense of self. He had never thought of himself as an introspective person; he was more inclined to focus on and complete tasks. Music was a task he did well. Taking care of the school was a set of tasks he did well. Tasks were tangible. They were items he could check off a to-do list. He hadn't thought of himself as a role model or an influencer. He had the mechanics of his life down pat. Everything else was outside his range of understanding. Now, he was being told that he had given a child a sense of purpose. What was his sense of purpose?

Flip's life had a assumed a comfortable rhythm: work every day except Thursdays and Sundays. He referred to Thursdays as slide whistle days; Saturdays as cleaning his one-bedroom apartment, work at school, and the band's gig days; Sundays as practice days with the band and often dinner at his parents. He dated from time to time, often meeting a woman at whatever gig his band played. There had been a few short-term relationships but nothing very serious. If asked, ex-girlfriends would describe Flip as well-groomed, courteous, musically talented, but without ambition. Amber once told her mother after dating Flip for several months that Flip was a nice guy with a quiet personality who never offends anyone. "But he never seems to really be listening when I talk to him. He's there but not really. I don't know if he has music in his head and not much else. I think I need to move on."

Flip did not pursue a rich social life. He enjoyed the comradery of the Quackers and the jazz band. He wasn't a loner, didn't feel alone, and was by no means a social outcast. He was more a listener without the need to engage in deep or lengthy conversation. Hearing Betty tell him about the effect he was having on her nephew Aaron changed Flip. He began observing the children of the Fiesta Band with a curiosity about others he had not previously experienced. He began asking questions. "How are things in Mrs. Parker's class? What are your favorite things to do besides play kazoo? Have you thought about learning to play another instrument? I wasn't the best student when I went to school here; how are you doing?"

His slide whistle and kazoo charges easily shared their thoughts and feelings. The relationship between Flip and what he began calling his "musical proteges" was very much a student/teacher relationship without the complications of lesson planning and issuing grades. Flip had discovered a purpose, which simplified his life.

Hannah's Triangle

It was the smallest home on the largest lot in a neighborhood of stately homes nestled among Japanese maples, sycamores and dogwoods with a half-acre of thoughtfully planned and maintained gardens. It was built well before the current trend of elaborate, look-at-me mansions. Hannah Parker lived among structures designed with spa-like bathrooms, immense kitchens with runway-sized marble islands, along with every imaginable electronic gadget snaked together by miles of wiring, which made those houses most vulnerable to international cyberattacks. Fortunately, Hannah's home was not vulnerable to outsiders, which made it a frequent gathering place for a diverse group of those whom Hannah called "influencers, intellectuals, and indigenous folk." She defined indigenous folk as being any interesting person she met while taking one of her daily walks.

Hannah grew up a child of privilege who eschewed the outward symbols of that privilege. Her husband Joe and daughter Deena found her propensity for bargain hunting both admirable and sometimes extreme. Hannah spent hours combing through the Sunday papers for coupons, which she categorized and saved in a large and sectioned accordion file folder. She lugged the binder with her on every shopping trip and liked to remind her husband and daughter, when she had chance to talk to her daughter who lived on the other side of the country, of the savings she had accumulated. She only bought furniture that was on sale and still subject to her bargaining skills. She seemed determined to not repeat the excesses of her parents, from whom she inherited a sizable estate, including her home that was once considered lavish for its time. While she did have a regular housekeeper and groundskeeper, she did not consider those luxuries; rather, she believed it was her duty to be an employer. And she paid twice the going hourly rate for both services. Other than Costco, she refused to knowingly shop at big box stores that mistreated their employees and harmed local, small businesses.

She was friendly but not social with her neighbors. They would describe her as the tall woman with flowing brown-going-to-elegant gray hair who walked quickly with the confidence of someone who always knew where they were going. She was usually dressed in khaki slacks and a white smock-like shirt and never wore anything but flats or comfortable sandals. She never applied make-up to her smooth, naturally rosy complexion. She cherished each age wrinkle as a sign of laughter and sadness, not unlike the Greek masks of comedy and tragedy.

Only a select few of her neighbors were aware of her Ivy-league education and doctorate in economics, a degree she used during a brief stint working for the United States Census Bureau as a statistical analyst. When she and her neighbors did interact, she was the one asking questions and listening, rarely offering an opinion or judgment. She had a way of making others feel comfortable by being interested in their lives. After she and Joe married, when they were both in their early thirties, they agreed that living in her inherited house would be best for raising their daughter who was born a few months after their wedding. Joe was a tax attorney with a successful practice where he worked with two other partners. Hannah was most proud of Joe's pro bono work with clients who believed they had been wronged by big government.

Hannah's secret pleasure was playing the triangle every Thursday morning with the Quackers at the city park's duck pond. Her friend Betty invited her into the group. At first Hannah declined, "I don't know anything about music. My daughter gave me a triangle for my birthday one year and I do enjoy its unique sound and resonance, but it's not a real instrument."

Betty convinced Hannah that the group was just for fun and even showed Hannah how to make several different sounds with the triangle. "It's a percussion instrument used to highlight certain musical sections and provide some rhythm. Give it a try. I'm the only one in the group who has any musical training. You'll have fun. Plus, it'll be another source of your real passion."

Initially, Hannah began showing up at the duck pond with triangle in hand and a bit of reluctance. Betty's support along with Buzzy's, who played a musical saw, helped her to feel part of the group without being essential. As the weeks wore on, Hannah became more and more enthusiastic, especially after mastering several rhythmic runs that required softer and louder beats on the triangle. She came to think of playing the triangle like clapping hands but with a better and more vibrant sound.

Hannah's real passion was hosting small, intimate gatherings for "smart debate and elevated understanding." She invited former university friends, work colleagues and acquaintances, as well as people she met at the duck pond or on her long walks about town. She was also an inveterate letter writer who peppered politicians, journalists, and other influencers with questions and invitations to her dinners.

There was the time she invited her old friend Hiram, a professor of philosophy from the local university, J. Patrick Moody, a self-professed voluntary street organizer who earned a living doing a variety of jobs whom she met while playing with The Quackers, and Ambrose "Amby" Morgan, the ultra-conservative state senator who happened to be the friend of a friend of a friend and to whom Hannah had written several letters asking about his stand on homelessness and what he planned to do about it.

Hannah's guests sat at the round kitchen table, the one she had grown up with, a solid oak table she had refinished in a dark mahogany stain and now covered with a red and white checkered oilcloth tablecloth. Hannah preferred functionality over style and, regardless of who sat at the table, it was easy to wipe a spill from vinyl. In the center of the table stood a small lazy Susan with salt and pepper shakers, several hot sauces, and extra napkins. Bottles of red and white wines were open, and, after brief introductions, Hannah encouraged her guests to pour themselves a glass while she finished arranging homemade dinner on family-style platters: roasted chicken, Israeli couscous, and a mix of root vegetables. Hannah never asked beforehand if her guests had dietary restrictions or preferences. She would say, "This is what I've made, enjoy or not." Hannah was not one to be easily offended if her dinner guests chose not to eat.

Hannah's husband was away at a legal conference. Hiram offered to help place the platters and serving utensils on the table. Hannah sat, poured herself a healthy glass of red wine, and invited everyone to serve themselves. "Leave room for dessert. I have an apple pie from Pop's."

J. Patrick Moody and Ambrose "Amby" Morgan sat quietly while Hannah and Hiram sipped a bit of wine. J. Patrick was dressed neatly in black jeans and a tan collared shirt with several cheap pens poking out of his breast pocket. He was in his early thirties with already thinning blond hair and he wore a serious expression. Ambrose "Amby" Morgan reclined with an overly relaxed posture; his coat jacket hung over the back of his chair and red suspenders accentuating a growing belly. His brown eyes moving quickly among the others with a clear hint of suspicion.

Amby broke the conversational ice by asking pointedly, "Hannah, why are we here?"

"For dinner and exploration. Hiram is a bit of a regular. Mr. Moody was kind enough to notice my triangle playing at the Duck Pond. And you, Amby, have taken several interesting political positions of late."

"Am I being set up?" asked Amby.

Hiram interjected, "No more than any of us. We set ourselves up anytime we take a position. Hannah offers us an opportunity to put aside our public personas and simply explore and seek to understand."

Hannah turned to J. Patrick Moody and asked, "Mr. Moody, what do you think?"

"Thanks for asking, but first, please just call me J. Pat. And I'm not sure what I think other than this is the best chicken I've ever had."

And so that's the way Hannah's dinners went. Several hours would pass with an air of politeness, often arrogant posturing, rarely any resolution and sometimes new friendships. The dinners were held every few months when Joe was away for business. He wasn't much for talking with strangers and definitely not one to engage in political haggling. When he returned home, however, he couldn't wait to ask Hannah about the dinners. They would sit over their own meals and Hannah would recount the evening's event flavoring it with her own judgments.

"I think Amby's I.Q. might be equal to his belt size, and he doesn't possess that much girth. He had the nerve to tell J. Pat that homelessness was the result of 'genetically induced' laziness. His actual words, not mine. Can you imagine such a doofus!"

Joe shook his head and said, "Sometimes I get a client who thinks paying taxes is the same as giving to the devil."

"Republicans? Evangelists?"

"Yes, as well as entitled and self-identified Liberals. And they're the same folks who don't believe in science or vaccines. They live their lives like those cheap slogans found on posters. I love the one that proclaims, 'Your inner voice is all you need. Trust the divine.' What sort of sanctimonious bullshit is the world coming to? They ought to hang signs on their extravagant mansions that say, 'My privilege makes me right.'"

Hannah laughed and replied, "Joe, I love you dearly and even more when you don't come to my dinners."

One Thursday morning Hannah joined the Quackers at the duck pond with her triangle in hand and a serious look. She had run into J. Pat on her walk. It had been several weeks since she had spent what turned out to be an overly tense dinner with him and pompous Amby. J. Pat left that dinner expressing his thanks for such a tasty meal and his regret that he had to endure all that was Amby.

"Hannah, I like to think of myself as a reasonable and open-minded person. I was grateful that you invited me to one of your dinners. You may or may not be aware that those you invite earn something of an elevated social status. Invitations to your dinners have gained a certain underground notoriety. I don't think that's what you wanted, but that's what's happening. And now you've, through no fault of your own, given Amby what he calls a "Blue Ribbon" to hang on his wall. His vanity wall with pictures of him with fellow politicians and other famous folks. I heard he framed your dinner invitation and hung it in a prominent place on his wall."

Hannah listened with concern, lips pursed, and brow furrowed. It was not her intent for the dinners to bring public attention to anyone. J. Pat just revealed an unintended consequence of her effort to build bridges and encourage common understanding among disparate groups.

"J. Pat, I've never asked, but what sort of work do you do? I just know you from those times you've watched us play at the duck pond and the brief conversations we had about the day's news. I found you to be a thoughtful person and that's why I invited you to dinner. I assumed you'd have an interesting perspective to add to our conversations."

"I do all sorts of things when I'm not volunteering. I guess you'd say I'm a gig worker. I'm an Uber driver and Instacart deliverer. I do a little freelance writing for the local newspaper and some travel publications. I do online tutoring, proofreading and editing for college students. I don't have any one job in particular." J. Pat stood straight with pride as he answered Hannah. It was an ongoing battle with his parents when they insisted that he settle into a career, and he argued that he wanted the independence to pick and choose what he wanted to do.

"You're making really interesting choices, J. Pat. We should all have so many options. Now you have me considering my own choices. Should I host dinners where the Amby's of the world might misuse them for their own self-promotion?"

The Quackers played a spirited rendition of "Oh, Susanna" that morning. Buzzy's saw never warbled truer and Betty strummed and plucked the zither with added enthusiasm. Hannah's mind was elsewhere, and she kept missing her beat. When Betty asked why she seemed so distracted, Hannah told her of how disturbed she felt after talking with J. Pat.

"Pompous men like Amby have a way of deeply hurting others and I'm convinced it's not accidental." Betty added in her own, self-styled crude manner of expressing herself, "Castration might be the only cure. And do it publicly! Nothing like a little open display of humiliation to cure buffoonery."

Hannah was used to Betty's politically incorrect language. She managed a neutral expression and said, "You do have a way, Betty."

The next day J. Pat phoned Hannah. He wished to apologize for his criticism of her dinners. He thanked Hannah for her good will and encouraged her to continue. "I realize that sometimes things don't go as planned, but I do admire your desire to bring diverse points of view into a room together. Besides, I can't forget the most delicious chicken I've ever had."

Hannah had answered her phone while immersed in her morning newspapers. She considered what J. Pat was saying, appreciated his kind words, but also felt a sense of ambiguity. "I appreciate your call, J. Pat. I've been thinking about what you said. I wonder if diversity is always a good thing. It seems that in your case in turned out to be a negative."

J. Pat responded, "But you really didn't host a dinner with true diversity. A few points of view aren't broad enough. You need to think about more than three or four dinner guests, otherwise it's just a case of taking sides."

That night Hannah served Joe halibut over orzo with a sweet chili sauce. They had several bites before Joe remarked, "This is really special. You rarely make fish and never with a sauce."

"It's a bottled sauce and the fish was on special."

Before dinner, Joe noticed that Hannah seemed to be lost in thought. She was not her normal communicative self. She didn't ask about Joe's day nor did she share anything about hers. Joe knew Hannah to be even-tempered and rarely moody, but he sensed that something was wrong.

"Okay, something has been bothering you for a while now. What's up?"

"I think I'm going to invite J. Pat and Amby back to dinner. I want you there, too."

"You know I don't want to be involved in your dinners. I'm proud of you for hosting them, but my job affords me enough daily conflict."

"But I need you this time."

Hannah described her ambiguous feelings about continuing to host her dinners. She didn't want to give license to anyone who might use them to cause harm to others or for their own ego-driven benefit. She could no longer fathom someone like Amby Morgan taking advantage to seemingly elevate his status.

Joe said, "You don't need me, Hannah. You need to trust your own instincts. Besides, you are much smarter than I."

Amby arrived wearing a three-piece, charcoal, pinstriped suit sporting a red and yellow paisley bow tie. He carried a bouquet of yellow roses and a broad grin as hubristic as his personality. Just as he entered, Hannah saw J. Pat emerge from his parked car and stride up her long entryway clothed in a much more relaxed manner, faded denim pants, black shirt and ecru-colored linen sport coat. Hannah noticed his freshly polished cordovan wingtips, which seemed a throwback to an earlier age. He carried a box of Sees nuts and chews, which he handed to Hannah along with a brief hug.

Amby was taken aback at J. Pat's and Hannah's familiarity. With raised eyebrows and a standoffish posture, he asked, "Am I being set up?"

Hannah replied, "It's just dinner. What would ever give you that impression?"

Mort, Micah, and Jordan Stories

Mort Gets a Thank-you

It was an overcast Tuesday in May. Low clouds hung over the valley's hills like a gray shroud threatening much-needed rain but yet to deliver. Winter had brought early hope and then reneged on breaking the three-year drought; the townsfolk now worshiped every rare drop that fell like unkept promises. The threat of a devastating fire was the topic of every regular coffee shop conversation, and there were an abundance of coffee shops in the small town nestled in the valley between two mountain ranges.

As he did every morning, Mort walked along Main Street on his way to his morning bagel and coffee at The Nosh and Kvetch Bagel Shop, known by regulars as N & K's. Medium height, slightly bent at the waist, he walked with a purpose honed after an almost forty-year career as a middle school English teacher. His retirement came just before cynicism set in and the bureaucracy became too much to bear. He was a relatively happy man with a noticeable paunch, glistening blue eyes, and always wearing a fisherman's cap covering thinning hair. If it was cold, he wore a Navy-blue pea coat; cool, a light jacket; warm or hot, a loud Hawaiian shirt.

He was always the first customer at N & K's and sat in the same booth in the far corner, the only one without a window, waiting for his longtime friend Al to arrive. Portia, a tall, elegant former ballet dancer, and owner of N & K's immediately came over and poured Mort a mug of first-of-the-morning coffee and told him his bialy with a schmear would be ready in a minute. She was one of the few African Americans in town and seemed to know as much, if not more, Yiddish as the Jews who frequented her shop. Mort and his friends found it a quaint anomaly and Portia laid claim to her knowledge as a result of growing up in South Philly.

After taking a sip of coffee and proclaiming it hot enough, Mort pulled a stack of plain, white notecards from his coat pocket and a well-used Pilot fountain pen from his shirt pocket and began writing his daily five thank-you notes to a variety of known and unknown people. He wrote notes to folks he read about in the newspaper or from stories he heard on the television news. To the boy who won the elementary school spelling bee; to the woman who knitted caps for soldiers; to the dog walker featured on the evening news who gave complimentary walks for those unable to exercise their furry friends; to any local who did something kind. He had always been a penner of notes. He made a habit to write notes to his students and their parents praising even the most minor of accomplishments. However, the notes he wrote while drinking coffee and munching on his bialy with a schmear were never sent. Instead, they were filed in three-by-five, plastic boxes, labeled by the year the notes were written, and neatly stored on his home office bookshelf next to a collection of obsolete teacher's editions of language arts textbooks.

Al strode in, waved at Portia, and sat across from Mort. If Mort was old school, fountain pen and note cards, Al was everything he thought modern: wearing a hipster hat, Nat Nast shirt, stylish jeans, whatever shoes teenagers flaunted and carrying the latest and most powerful smart phone currently available. None of it made any sense to Mort, who thought his friend of almost forty years was a bit daft for donning clothes that looked silly on a balding, six foot five, ectomorph with very little muscle tone who walked with a slouch and had no idea how to take full advantage of the electronic power he held in his left hand. Mort thought of Al as a billboard for how not to grow old with dignity. Yet, Al was the one friend to whom he could confide his deepest secrets ever since they met as first-year teachers.

Portia set a steaming cup of chai before Al, glanced at his new fedora, and suggested the lox and onion omelet.

"That would be perfecto," said Al. "And how's your Brutus today?" referring to Portia's husband Tom who did the cooking and never engaged with the customers.

"Oh, you know, conspiring as always," replied Portia with a smile before turning and heading to a table where another group of regulars sat.

"I see you've got a nice stack of thank-you notes that will never be sent."

"It's the thought that counts," replied Mort with his usual cliché. He lowered his voice and said, "Al, the strangest thing happened on my walk over this morning."

Mort described how an unknown person ran up behind him and pushed a card into his coat pocket before running away. "All of a sudden I felt a hand in my pocket and this person dressed in all black and wearing a hoodie run off. I couldn't tell if it was a man or a woman. I pulled this card out of my pocket." Mort showed Al the card which read, "You changed my life."

"Well, at least someone out there believes in delivering thank-you notes."

"You're assuming it's a thank-you note."

Portia set Al's omelet down and refilled the coffee cups. Al took a bite and proclaimed it excellent. "Tell me again, Portia, how does a beautiful Black woman from South Philly who knows more about being Jewish than Mort or moi own a bagel shop?"

Portia replied as she did every time Al asked, "Ethiopia by way of Israel with a dose of Philly culture as my guide."

And Al sang, as he always did when he and Portia engaged in banter, "We are the world, we are the children, we are the ones who make a brighter day."

"So true, Al."

"And yet it all comes down to bagels," laughed Al.

"And the kvetch."

Al examined the card, which was mysteriously put into Mort's pocket, and suggested it was from a woman. Mort asked how he could tell and Al said the block printed letters had a certain flourish making the writing more of a feminine hand. "Besides, I don't think men write in orange ink. I think what you have is a secret admirer." Al returned the card to Mort and paid closer attention to his omelet.

"I doubt that. Besides Effie is the only admirer I need." Effie was Mort's wife of over thirty-five years. She was a Rubenesque woman of sturdy stature, bawdy laugh, and a stove that produced meals fit for a dozen even when it was just she and Mort for dinner. Their four grown children, two sons and two daughters, made a habit of dropping by unannounced during mealtime knowing there would be plenty for themselves and the grandchildren. Their kids had a way of communicating with each other so that only one family 'came by out of the blue' at a time. Two or three times a week, the front door of their home would open just before the 5:30 dinnertime, and Effie would exclaim, "What a nice surprise! I'll set the table for guests." Then she would wrap her fleshy arms around each son or daughter and the grandchildren, pull them down to her level and kiss each of them on the forehead, before moving the two place settings from the kitchen table to the dining room table and arranging additional settings. Mort always shook his head knowingly and directed his son or daughter to open a bottle of the good wine and then inform him of how they happened to drop by. The stories were always creative and Mort relished the fiction.

Al remarked, "One can never have too many admirers. It's like having a blood bank for the soul."

"I think you mean friends," said Mort.

"Perhaps."

Before leaving, Mort and Al made it a point to wave at Portia and point to the cash they had left on the table, which always included a generous tip and a thank-you note from Mort. Unlike the notes he would file when he got home, it was the only note Mort delivered and he always wrote, "Thank you for giving my day such a good start. You're the best!" What Mort didn't know was that Portia would deposit each note in a plastic garbage bag labeled "Mort's Notes" which hung in the utility closet in the rear of the kitchen. When asked by the custodians who cleaned after hours why she kept them, she easily replied, "He's a rare bird and I'm not about to discard a nice gesture."

The next morning, Mort was extra alert and cautious as made his regular walk. He looked from side-to-side, pausing a few times before entering the N & K. Portia held a pot of coffee in his direction and nodded towards his table. As he began to scoot into his booth, he noticed a card on the seat. He picked it up, turned it over, and read, "Seriously, you changed my life."

Portia came over with a heavy ceramic mug and poured him coffee. "Another note, Mort?"

"It was on the seat. Did you see who put it there?"

"As always, you're the first one in," said Portia. "I have no idea how it got there. I'll get your bialy ready."

Mort examined the card. It was printed in the same orange block letters as the first one, clearly by the same hand. The card was identical to the ones Mort used. He wondered who might have written the notes. A former student? Someone with a grudge? Someone simply playing mind games? Mort never saw himself as a popular teacher among his students, or one who received elevated respect from colleagues. For holidays, other teachers often received thoughtful and sometimes extravagant gifts. Al was an idolized math teacher and carried boxes of gifts to his car before winter and spring breaks and even more boxes before summer vacation. Mort was given few and usually just a holiday card from a smattering of students. Mort thought of himself as a journeyman who skillfully taught his students the required curriculum without any special flourish. While known for his frequent thank-you notes, most of his students viewed him as old-fashioned and out of touch with popular topics and current events.

"This was here when I arrived," said Mort showing the card to Al who arrived earlier than usual and before Mort had a chance to begin writing new thank-you notes. "I think I'm being stalked. Who would want to harass me?"

Al took the card and remarked sardonically, "Having a stalker might be the greatest compliment you've ever received."

Portia approached with Mort's bialy, a coffee pot, and a mug for Al. "I think I'll change things up this morning, Portia. How about black tea and a ham and cheese omelet?"

"You know we don't have ham, Al."

"All of a sudden you're kosher?" questioned Al. "Has the world flip-flopped?"

"No, we just don't have ham. We do have Canadian bacon and regular bacon. No ham." Portia stood before Al with her perfect posture, unblemished café au lait skin, and a close-lipped smile that projected mirth and patience.

"What difference does it make?"

"It's what sells, Al. We don't sell ham. No demand. We don't have pork chops either," Portia remarked now with a toothy smile and a wink toward Mort, who understood her jest."

"I think Ethiopia created a lost tribe that's still trying to find its way," said Al. "Okay, I'll go with a Canadian bacon and Swiss cheese omelet with a toasted plain bagel. Oh, and regular hash browns, not that souped up version with all the onions and peppers."

Portia quickly returned with Al's tea and mentioned, "The cook salutes you, Al."

Al handed the card back to Mort who had been enjoying, as he always did, the banter between Al and Portia. He also knew that ham was available, because, unlike Al, from time to time he read the menu. He knew that Portia playfully refused it to Al and that Al enjoyed Portia's denials.

Al suggested that Mort's secret stalker was probably Portia. Al said that he would have known if it was Portia when the runner placed the card in his pocket. "Besides, Portia was already here when I arrived. No, it must be someone with a grudge. Perhaps, a former student who earned a poor grade."

"People with grudges don't write 'you changed my life' notes.

"I don't think I was ever a life changer."

Al asked Mort if he knew about the butterfly effect. He explained how the flapping of a butterfly's wings in Asia could impact the weather in North America. "Tiny actions can create massive results. Your small teacher acts may have caused a tsunamic effect for someone else."

"I doubt I ever caused more than a ripple, much less a high tide."

Portia returned with Al's omelet. "Here's your ham and cheese omelet with your boring bagel and even more boring potatoes. The cook made a special run to Safeway for your ham."

"Many thanks for the service. I'll be sure to return tomorrow," laughed Al. "Big tip today!" he added with a flourish.

Later that day, Al told Effie about the first and second notes. Effie listened before informing Mort what she found on the windshield of their fifteen-year-old Prius, which had been driven less than 50,000 miles. Effie and Mort rarely took vacations by car; they hardly vacationed at all. Their children had given them an anniversary gift of two weeks in New York City with arrangements for them to see a play or musical production every day they were there. There was the one trip to Israel with a group from their synagogue shortly after Mort's retirement. Portia had been an invaluable source of travel information, which they used well on those few open days on their tour's itinerary. For example, where to taste the best shawarma, tastiest falafel, and how to bargain for jewelry at the markets in Old Jerusalem. Although Portia had grown up in Pennsylvania, she and her family often visited relatives in Israel and, after graduating from high school and enrolling at Penn on a full scholarship, she spent a gap year living with an aunt and cousins in Tel Aviv.

Effie continued to listen as Mort described how the cards were delivered, one surreptitiously by an anonymous runner and the other left on his booth's seat for him to find. They sat opposite one another in matching wingback chairs that had become saggy and slightly threadbare. Mort sat low with his legs crossed. When Effie sat, she appeared as tall as she was wide, like a cuddly stuffed bear wedged into the chair.

"Al thinks it's a female's handwriting, but it's hard to tell." He showed the cards to Effie who agreed that block printing made it difficult to identify gender. "It's so strange, Effie. What do you think?"

Effie considered the two cards: 'You changed my life' and 'Seriously, you changed my life.' "I wonder why there is increased emphasis in the second card. Everyone takes you seriously. I think that's why Al is such a good friend. Nobody takes him seriously," gushed Effie with a laugh so loud and only tolerated by her family and friends. "I wouldn't make much of it. It's nice to know that someone out there is so appreciative of you. And, by the way, there was a third card. I found in on the car's windshield this morning." Effie pulled the card from her apron's pocket and handed it to Mort. It read in bright orange ink, 'So thankful you changed my life.'

"This was on the windshield while the car was parked in the garage?" asked Mort with a measure of disbelief.

"Yes, I found it this morning while getting some laundry detergent."

"In the garage where the side door is always locked and I can't remember the last time the garage door was open."

Effie thought for a moment, her eyes closed and her fingers drumming her lap. "How could that be?"

Mort rose from his chair with a trace of a grunt and walked to the kitchen and through the door leading into the garage. He checked to see if the outside door was locked and found that it was and without any sign of it being forced open. He returned to the living room chair and sat with another trace of a grunt and told Effie that the garage was secure.

"You're sure the garage door was not left open for a while when you were doing something else?"

"We haven't driven the car in over a week, the last time we went grocery shopping. There's been no reason to open the door."

"This is very strange. I'm not sure what to make of this," said Mort while tugging at his right ear, a habit he had developed when trying to think things through.

Effie pointed at Mort and with her usual loud, but loving tone said, "Someone simply admires and appreciates you. Now, I need to get dinner going. I have a feeling we'll have company tonight." She rose from her chair without a sound and headed into the kitchen. Mort remained sitting like a confused puppy needing direction from his trainer.

Mort slipped into his booth, waved at Portia who was tending to another early morning patron, and felt relief that there were no new notes to be discovered and surprised that he was not the first customer. He took out a short stack of notecards and his fountain pen and wrote his first thank-you of the day, "Thank you, whomever you are, for not mysteriously leaving me a card today. I hope you will reveal yourself soon."

Portia set a hot mug of coffee before Mort, confirmed his usual order, and turned to find Al standing next to her smiling like someone with a secret that wouldn't be shared.

"How's the beautiful Ethiopian Jewess this morning?"

"You know, Al, your advancing years does not give you license to be so grossly inappropriate."

"I apologize for being in awe of such a divine creature as yourself. And one of my culture, to boot."

Portia paused with a pot of coffee in one hand and the other on her hip. "You know very little of my culture and I doubt much of your own, Al. Plain bagel and a lox scramble today?"

"Sounds good. And it may surprise you that I might know more than either you or Mort."

Mort watched this exchange feeling a shiver of shame for his friendship with Al and a lot of respect for Portia's ability to stand her ground without sarcasm or contrived attitude.

"Another card was left on my car's windshield while it was parked in our locked garage," said Mort with obvious distress in his voice. "Who and how did someone get in my garage? Effie found it. She doesn't think it's a big deal. She says I have a secret admirer."

"One of your kids, maybe," suggested Al. "Or perhaps a grandchild. Or maybe Portia, she seems to have taken a liking to you." Al looked at the card that Mort had written to his anonymous writer. "Now, this one is truly undeliverable and not worth the energy you are putting into it."

"I don't know what else to do."

"Just accept the fact that you had a positive impact on a former student and let it be."

Several weeks passed without any more secret notes. Mort kept to the usual rhythm of his days, writing thank-you notes, meeting Al at N & K's for his usual coffee and bialy with a schmear, Al's feigning alarm at not being able to order a ham and cheese omelet and then being served one by the elegant Portia who always remarked with reserved sarcasm, "he ran over to Safeway to buy ham just for you, Al," and the ambiguity he felt over Al's inappropriate speech with Portia.

One day he was sipping his coffee and enjoying his bialy with a schmear. He began writing a thank-you note to a good Samaritan he had spotted picking up dog poop after an inconsiderate dog walker failed to do so when Portia slid into the side of the booth reserved for Al. Her face was serious like those frequent times one of his former students would approach with the news that he had lost his homework assignment and was hoping to be given an extension, which Mort always granted.

"Mort, I need to ask, how many years have you been coming here every morning, ordering the same thing, writing thank-you notes, kibbitzing with Al, and then leaving a generous tip and a thank-you note?"

"I think about three years."

"Well, today's note will make it an even 800. I know this because I've kept and counted all the cards, all the cards with exactly the same message. When you consider we are closed on Sundays and on major holidays and those few weeks I've taken for vacations, it's been a little over three years. I appreciate the tips and the notes. By the way, I can put up with Al's idiotic talk, which I take mostly as an alter kacker's feeble attempt at charm, however misplaced. But why the undelivered notes. I've never asked, but after three years I want to know."

Mort sat like a contrite poodle who knew he did something wrong but wasn't sure what. He looked at Portia for a moment before wiping his lips with a napkin and clearing his throat.

"I've never been asked. My wife thinks it's cute. Al believes I'm simply meshuga. I'm surprised that you've kept all the notes. So, I'll tell you why."

It felt unusually quiet inside the Nosh & Kvetch. All the other booths were empty and Al had yet to arrive. Portia's face had changed from overly serious to more neutral anticipation.

"It's all about gratitude," said Mort.

"Gratitude."

"Yes, gratitude. I once read about the benefits of keeping a gratitude journal. How the daily affirmation of gratitude could be life enriching. I've never been much for New Age philosophy, but I was struck by the notion of a personal exclamation of gratitude, or, in my case, thankfulness. When

I was a teacher, I had always written thank-you notes to my students. I think they thought it was corny and I'm sure they ended up in the trash without a second thought. I'm sure I wrote those notes as a way of somehow controlling their behavior or at least trying to use praise to encourage repeated good deeds. I realize I expected something in return for saying thanks. Now I write notes to remind me of how much I have to be thankful for without expecting anything in return."

"Then why am I the only one who gets a note?"

"I think it's because you go out of your way to make me feel special every day. And, of course, you go out of your way to irritate Al with your 'he ran over to Safeway to get your ham' remark.

The N & K's door opened and Al walked in and approached. Before sliding out of the booth to make room for Al, Portia leaned across the table and whispered, "You've changed my life, Mort."

"You're the secret note writer," said Mort with relief.

"No. I'm not."

Micah Decides

"I decided to think of it as a period of training in techniques for dealing with boredom."

Norwegian Wood
Haruki Murakami

There's a tiny neighborhood park with a koi pond, where fish and frogs flourish, filled with too many lilies and surrounded by rhododendrons, cottonwoods, and birch. Three benches are situated around the pond with *Don't Feed the Ducks* signs prominently displayed adjacent to each bench. Ducks haven't used the pond for years; few people take advantage of the benches. This lush space is surrounded by a strip of lawn, which is largely unused because it lacks the space for lawn games and is too visible by passersby for intimacy. It's not like the other popular park in the middle of town that attracts residents and visitors with its hundreds of acres of lawns, ponds, playgrounds, and specialty gardens. This small park is officially named Polk Street Park. The few folks who use it, mostly senior citizens looking for a quiet reprieve, refer to it as The Pond and consider it an afterthought by a city council that believes small neighborhoods deserve small parks.

Most mornings just after sunrise, Micah sits on one of the benches with a journal and pen in hand looking for inspiration. He begins with closed eyes and five minutes of meditation, trying to clear his mind of all thoughts before opening his eyes searching for something he hadn't seen before. He once read a quote by Monet, 'Aside from painting and gardening, I am good for nothing.' Like Monet, he thought aside from seeking daily insight and maybe a story, I'm good for nothing. Once a moderately successful writer of young adult fiction, he had been coming to the same bench every morning trying to find a story. His journal largely remained blank with infrequent descriptions of familiar koi moving among the lily pads and frogs leaping from rocks to water.

The morning moon hung low in a cloudless sky on this particular day. Micah, short pudgy and gnomish, slowly walked to his bench. He wore a baggy grey hoodie, oversized black sweatpants, and Birkenstock sandals with brown socks. The morning was cool and still. Micah sat and heard a flurry of frogs seeking shelter and noticed two koi moving through the lilies like miniature submarines. Just as he closed his eyes he heard a loud grunt from outside the circle of lush growth surrounding the pond. At first, he felt a shiver of alarm but gave it no heed and kept his eyes shut against any distraction from his meditation.

Micah learned at an early age to maintain distance. The day he turned nine, his father was driving him to his favorite ice cream store for his special birthday sundae, butter brickle ice cream with butterscotch topping and two cherries on top. They came upon a bicyclist, about Micah's age, who was sitting on the curb next to his bike crying and holding a hand to his bloody forehead. It was obvious the boy had fallen and appeared to be in distress. Micah stared as his father drove by and admonished him to look away and told him there was nothing they could do. This became standard practice: look away and ignore. Every time he witnessed someone needing assistance, he never offered help and it felt unnatural like a menthol eucalyptus lozenge lodged in his throat. As a teenager, he began writing about his inability to reach out and his constant feeling of isolation. He had short stories published before turning eighteen and a moderately successful novella in his early twenties. He found an agent and editor who encouraged him to write more young adult fiction and he churned out three *Jonah Stands Alone* novels in four years with the prospect of turning the most popular one into a movie or limited television series. It's been over twenty years and still no movie or series. And only one more book, a stab at more adult themes, which hardly sold, went to remainder shelves almost immediately upon release. It resulted in his losing his publisher and rare communication with his agent. *Jonah Stands Alone* continues to sell, especially translated copies in Europe and Japan, and, although the royalties are modest, they're enough to keep him financially afloat.

Opening his eyes, Micah looked into the pond wondering what mysteries might be found there. Were there coins thrown in by wish makers? What were the wishes? Lost keys to hidden treasures? What sort of locks might those keys open? What treasures might be discovered? A story waiting to be told? In the pervading quiet and chilly fog which had rolled in like an unwelcomed blanket, he opened his journal and wrote: another day begins without substance. He closed his journal and placed it and his pen in his sweatshirt's pouch pocket and stood to walk home. As he emerged from the embrace of shrubs and trees surrounding the pond and began to cross the narrow strip of lawn towards the sidewalk, he saw a young man slumped over on his knees and gasping for breath.

His first inclination was to turn away and walk home, perhaps with a brisker pace than usual. He eyed the stranger who appeared to be in his twenties, wearing a long-sleeved, purple T-shirt, green Nike sweatpants, and fluorescent orange running shoes. Micah thought this stranger, with long black hair that covered his face, must be a jogger suffering from severe cramping. It would have been enough of an excuse to continue moving along but then the man coughed and vomited before letting out guttural moan. Micah became transfixed and unable to walk forward.

The young man, with spittle dripping off his chin, looked up at Micah. Micah saw his face, oval and pasty with deep blue eyes pleading for help. He sat back on his haunches, wrapping his arms around his knees, and pulling them close to his chest before rolling over on his side.

They were seated at Micah's kitchen table drinking hot tea. By the time Micah had helped the young man to his feet and walked him home, he learned that his name was Jordan and that he lived nearby. Micah kept an arm around Jordan's back during the three-block walk. There was little conversation other than Micah reassuring Jordan that he was merely trying to help. Jordan walked haltingly, clutching at his midsection from time to time. He was much taller than Micah but pitched over and holding his stomach walked at the same height. He kept muttering that he didn't know what had happened and thanked Micah for his assistance.

After sipping tea for about fifteen minutes, Jordan was able to sit up straighter on the vinyl covered chair, his elbows on the table and staring into the mug of black tea. He looked up and asked, "How did I get here?"

"Should I call someone? Do you need to go to a hospital?"

"The tea helps and I think I'm okay. What happened to me?"

"I found you keeled over in the park. I don't know why and I'm not even sure I did the right thing, but I thought it best to walk you to my house. I didn't have a cell phone with me, so I couldn't call anyone. I think I'm maybe as confused about all of this as you."

"All I remember is being out for my morning run and suddenly feeling something hitting me in the stomach. It felt like I had run into something at full speed."

Micah asked Jordan to pull up his shirt. There was the beginning of a baseball bat shaped bruise forming across his midsection, red surrounded by a bluish tint. "Are you able to take a deep breath without pain?"

Jordon inhaled into his stomach and slowly exhaled. "Sore and a bit uncomfortable. I've broken a rib before and it doesn't feel that way. I definitely ran into something."

"Or something ran into you," said Micah.

"Are you a doctor or a nurse or some kind of medical person?"

"No. I just read a lot. I'm a writer. Maybe I ought to get you an ice pack."

Micah filled a plastic baggie with ice, wrapped it in a tea towel, and handed it to Jordan. Jordan pulled up his shirt and held the ice pack against his stomach with a short wince.

"Maybe you ought to use it on the outside of your shirt," suggested Micah.

Jordan smiled and said, "I think you're right. He sat holding the ice pack in his left hand and sipping tea with his right. "Are you the neighborhood good Samaritan?"

"This is first time I've ever helped anyone," said Micah with a soft, tentative voice. "Should anyone be contacted? Are you married, or have a roommate, or live at home with family?"

Several weeks went by before Micah saw Jordan again. During that interval, Micah continued his daily routine, a dawn walk to the pond with meditation and no new story ideas. He was on his way home when Jordan came jogging toward him. Micah waved in recognition and Jordan stopped. He had been running for a while and he stood tall, his face aglow with soft perspiration, yet his breathing was unstressed. Micah said that he looked healthy and back to normal; Jordan thanked him, again, for his kindness. He told Micah that, other than a bruise which was largely gone, he felt fine.

"I wonder what really happened to you that morning. Do you think someone attacked you?"

Jordan replied, "I haven't the foggiest idea. When I run, I often go into a trancelike state and don't have an awareness of my surroundings."

"Don't you worry about traffic?"

"That's why I run early. And I always take the same route. I've had cars honk at me a few times and that alerts me."

"You need to be careful," advised Micah paternalistically.

Jordan continued on his run and Micah walked home thinking about his father. He thought about all those times when his father instructed him to look away and pretend there was nothing they could do. It was surprising how many times that occurred. It was not only the boy who fell from his bike but also the time they walked by a homeless woman curled up in an abandoned shop doorway shivering and crying for help. His father pushing him along, telling him not to look and saying there was nothing they could do for someone who doesn't want to take care of themselves. There was another time when they witnessed a car accident on the freeway and his father swerved to avoid the car that had rolled over. Micah could see the driver and passenger hanging upside down from their seatbelts while his father sped off saying others were stopping to help. Micah used those instances to write stories about young people who performed heroic acts. His best-selling book was about a teenager who pulled a driver from a flipped automobile just before the car burst into flames.

Micah could take action in his imagination but not when it counted, which made helping Jordan remarkable. He found himself perseverating about his new out-of-character behavior. While morning meditation failed to yield story ideas, he began to outline a new book based on what he felt was his own transformation from meek bystander to a self-professed man of action. As he emerged from his writing rut, he found himself looking for opportunities to help others. He wanted more proof that he had indeed changed. One day he was at the grocery store when an elderly woman shopping in the dairy aisle slipped on a recently mopped floor. A few other shoppers watched as Micah rushed over, helped the woman to her feet, and asked if she was okay. She thanked Micah for being her hero and assured him she was fine. A hero thought Micah. He wrote in his journal, 'how could I possibly be anyone's hero?' The working title of his new book was *Crossing Jordan: A Hero's Journey.*

Micah called Jordan to ask his permission to use his name in the title of his new book. Jordan told Micah he felt complimented and wanted to know more about Micah's story. They decided to meet for breakfast the next morning. Micah was already seated in a both at The Nosh and Kvetch Bagel Shop when Jordan arrived still wearing his jogging gear. Jordan acknowledged Micah with a wave, walked past his booth, and stopped at the last booth to say hello to his former English teacher Mort Rothman. He remembered Mr. Rothman as the only teacher who ever wrote him a thank you note. They exchanged a few quiet words before Jordan walked back and slid into the seat across from Micah. Portia, who owned the shop with her husband, approached with a pot of coffee and two white ceramic mugs. Micah and Jordan thanked her for coffee and both ordered bagels with lox and cream cheese.

"No capers or tomatoes for me," said Micah.

"The works for me," said Jordan. "Also, a scrambled egg and hash browns."

"Loading up on carbs, Jordan?" asked Portia.

"Always."

Portia left to tend to other diners and Micah asked, "Are you a regular here?"

"Only before or after a longer than usual run. Portia knows when I'm carbo loading."

Micah nodded, "I think I'll use that in the story I'm writing."

Jordan took a long swig of coffee waiting for Micah to continue. Jordan always had flexible morning time. He managed a local hardware store and worked the noon to eight shift, which gave him the time for morning workouts and the opportunity to work at developing his online business buying and selling vintage fountain pens. It was something in which he became interested after Mr. Rothman told him how much he valued writing with his cherished Pilot fountain pen. Mostly he bought old, broken pens and had taught himself how to restore them for resale. YouTube had become an invaluable reference.

"Micah, I checked you out on the internet. You wrote several successful young adult books but it's been a long time since you've published anything. What now? Why me? You hardly know me. Aren't writers supposed to write about what they know and from their own experience."

Portia served their food and refilled their coffee mugs. Micah thanked her, took a bite of his bagel and lox, and pensively thought about what Jordan had asked. The three Jonah novels were rooted in his own experiences. Writing about loneliness and feelings of disconnectedness were very much something he knew well. He could not explain his coming to Jordan's aid, assisting elderly ladies, or his newfound desire to take action like a "hero." He didn't believe that any of those actions were bold enough to be considered heroic. Perhaps, the hero's journey he was writing about was more about transformative behaviors. Perhaps, the change from disconnected to connected was a heroic process.

"Good question, Jordan. I think writers are supposed to know what they write about, not necessarily what they know from their own experience. Knowing is a process of discovery. And writers can learn in a variety of ways."

"Why use my name in the title? I'm certainly not a hero."

"You represent the first time I ever stepped forward to help someone in distress. I'm not saying I was being heroic but it's caused me to think of writing a story which is about what it means to be a hero. I know it's a common theme, but this story is intended to tell how the hero of the story changes from living in a rut to a life meaningfully lived.

"Sounds like a retelling of *The Odyssey,*" said Jordan.

"You've read *The Odyssey*?"

"No, but I saw *Oh, Brother, Where Art Thou.*"

Micah laughed open-mouthed and spewed a spray of coffee into his open hand. He used his napkin to tidy up and said, "So many ways to enjoy the classics."

Jordan stared back with an expression that wondered if Micah was being sarcastic or complimentary. Micah quickly realized Jordan's confused concern and clarified by telling him that modern retellings were good for knowing classical literature. He added that "Oh, Brother" was one of his favorite movies.

"Why my name in the title?"

"Because you were the beginning of my new journey."

Micah's early morning routine remained. However, his meditations took on a new focus. Instead of hoping for inspiration, he used the time to simply quiet his mind. It's what he had always attempted to do but found himself thinking rather than trying not to. He no longer had an expectation of new ideas. He sat placidly allowing the morning to come to him, the cool temperatures, sometimes fog, the sounds of frogs and birds, the ripple of koi languidly moving through the lily pond. He welcomed what nature offered as sensory gifts and not as intrusions. His meditation time expanded from five to ten minutes. He didn't think about his new writing until he returned home and sat before his computer with a daily dose of renewal. He had metamorphosed from being a writer when it was convenient to a disciplined writer who wrote for at least four hours every day. He finished the first draft in six months, sent it to his agent, and called Jordan asking him if he'd like to read it.

Micah anticipated good news, as his agent had asked him several times for a novel geared to adult tastes. After sending off the draft, he gave himself permission to take a break from writing. He decided to work on getting himself into better physical shape. If he was going to be more of a man of action, he thought it best not to be a pudgy one. He began by taking longer walks and dining less at N & K's. It would take time to rid himself of the bagel bulge he had accumulated. He admired Jordan's commitment to daily runs but running was not in his repertoire. Instead, he worked at becoming a faster walker, moving his short legs like an upturned turtle. In just a few weeks, he felt his body changing. He began keeping a daily diary using his phones health application to document his walking distances and times. He gave up the occasional evening cigar and switched to fresh fruit and green tea.

"It's an interesting first draft, Micah. Very different. But there's lots more work to be done," his agent informed him with her usual clipped voice. "I don't feel connected to your character. Your writing lacks the passion of your other novels. I want you to care more about Jordan. What makes this story different from other heroic journeys? I've made extensive notes on the draft and will mail it back to you. There's promise here but you'll need to decide how to move forward."

Micah thanked his agent for her feedback and said he'd look forward to reading her notes before getting back to her. Micah was determined to maintain a sanguine outlook. He felt there were choices to be made even when the message was not what he hoped. He could be sad, angry, defeated, stoic or positive. He chose optimistic and would assess next steps after getting back the marked-up draft.

It was another cool, foggy morning at The Pond. A light breeze hushed through the trees and, when Micah crossed the dewy lawn, he could feel the chill through his sandals. He sat on a bench and began to meditate. He had now extended his time for what he called "the contemplation of emptiness" to fifteen minutes. When he opened his eyes, he noticed a koi facing him and softly swaying its body like a metronome for a waltz tempo. Sitting next to him was Jordan.

"Good morning, Jordan. You managed to come without me noticing. Thanks so much for taking the time to meet me here. I'm interested in knowing what you thought about my story."

"I like it but also agree with your editor's comments. What are you thinking of doing?"

Micah placed his hand on Jordan's shoulder. "I appreciate your kindness and most of all your friendship. These last months have been helpful to my own journey. And now I know what I need to do."

"And what will you do?" asked Jordan.

"I will decide."

Jordan

Buying, repairing, and selling fountain pens is a niche hobby with lots of joy and rarely any profit. There is a surprisingly large community of self-described pen nerds who spend time online searching for an unusual, not necessarily rare, find. Like stamp collectors who fill albums with the common and the occasional less-than-common stamp, most pen collectors own a wide array while peppering their collections with limited editions. An even smaller subset of pen collectors purchase vintage pens in need of repair and restoration. Many send their pens to professional restorers, while others learn how to complete their own renovations, which they keep for their own cherished collections. And then there are a very select few who seek out pens in need of repair, who restore and resell them.

Jordan didn't know anything about fountain pens until he observed his eighth-grade English teacher Mr. Rothman using one to write a note. It was the first time he became aware of the existence of fountain pens. Throwaway Bic ballpoints or Paper Mate Flair felt tip pens and Ticonderoga pencils were the only writing implements he knew. Watching Mr. Rothman use his Pilot fountain pen to write a thank-you note was a unique experience. The delicate flow of ink, letters finished with a flourish, a gentle blow of air to dry the cursive letters were so captivating that it changed Jordan's life. He began to research the history of fountain pens and the variety of pens available for purchase. The public library had several books on the subject and the internet was an endless resource. Because of Mr. Rothman, Jordan had discovered a passion.

Jordan was not a popular adolescent. He had a few friends who enjoyed running, something Jordan had been doing with his father since fifth grade. Every morning before breakfast and getting ready for school, he and his father ran a route from their home, past Polk Street Park and back. Tall and lanky like his father, they ran with long, easy strides for several miles without ever being out of breath. Running and fountain pens became a lifelong pursuit; lifelong, so far, being in his twenties, managing his father's hardware store, and dabbling in an online pen business.

He had just finished a brisk 10K run and stopped at the Nosh & Kvetch Bagel Shop for breakfast. He ordered a large apple juice, Spanish omelet and sesame bagel from Portia, the elegant Ethiopian Jew who owned the diner with her husband, who did the cooking. After eating, while checking for emails, Facebook posts, and news on his cell phone, he would walk home to spend an hour or so posting on his personal website the latest restored pens he had for sale. He was very proud of the1940's Eversharp Skyline fountain pen he had just finished polishing after replacing the ink sac. Purchased for $10, he would list it on Etsy for $120. He was reading an email from a prospective pen purchaser when his former middle school math teacher walked in and doffed his fedora towards Portia with an enthusiastic 'shalom.' Mr. Al, the name he insisted students call him after a popular Paul Simon song, strode over to the last booth and sat with his old friend Mort Rothman.

Jordan thought of Mr. Rothman and Mr. Al as quite an odd pair. He knew that Mr. Rothman was very much like himself, not being one of the popular teachers. Although his students respected him for his serious approach and the thank-you notes he frequently churned out, he wasn't the teacher who received extravagant holiday gifts or any other special recognition. They thought of him as a kind, frumpy teacher who taught the book without much creativity. Mr. Al, on the other hand, was very popular. He made math fun with lots of games for teaching hard concepts and for his easy availability at lunch and after school to help students. He insisted that his students pass his classes and goaded students with humor to keep persisting through difficult problems. His favorite line with girls was, "Don't let being a girl keep you from being a mathematician." His favorite with the boys, "Language counts and don't let being a boy keep you from explaining your proofs." Students didn't know what he meant by either expression but knew he cared and they responded to Mr. Al who dressed like them and tried using their vernacular.

Jordan looked up from his phone and watched Mr. Rothman and Mr. Al in conversation. Mr. Rothman listening with quiet eyes and Mr. Al waving his hands to emphasize whatever he was saying. Although Mr. Al was loud much of the time, his interactions with Mr. Rothman were always vocally subdued and punctuated by extravagant gesturing. As popular as Mr. Al had been in middle school, Jordan was still drawn more to Mr. Rothman. It was more than his growing fascination with fountain pens. Mr. Rothman showed a quiet dignity when using his Pilot pen and it captured Jordan's imagination. Jordan treasured the thank-you notes Mr. Rothman had written to him and his parents. His mother had framed the one that said, 'Thank you for being you. Being true to oneself is never taken for granted.' It was well after high school when Jordan realized the influence Mr. Rothman had on his life.

It had been over a year since Micah had come to Jordan's aid, finding him slumped over on the lawn near the pond where he meditated most mornings. Micah's kindness and subsequent sharing of his new novel had forged an unlikely friendship. Micah was about twice Jordan's age, lived a reclusive life, and from what Jordan could determine, had virtually no social life. Jordan's work required ongoing social interactions and, in his off time, he enjoyed running and a busy social life with a few close friends. In common, they were both early morning people, Micah meditating by the pond shortly after dawn and Jordan out for his 10K run. Ever since Micah had shared the first draft of his new novel with Jordan, their friendship had grown and they met several times a month for breakfast and N & K's.

Micah always arrived before Jordan. Wearing a loose-fitting hoodie and sweatpants, Micah sipped coffee and thought about the rewrite *The Hero Within*, formerly titled *Crossing Jordan: A Hero's Journey.* He took to heart the feedback about his first draft and realized his story needed to probe deeper into the soul of his heroic character. He was told his story lacked personal passion. Now, he labored at developing a character with whom others would feel a connection. Much like his own journey of self-discovery, he was writing a story that shifted from doing deeds to finding the hero within. Micah had been on his own journey of finding his true self. He no longer intentionally disconnected from others in their time of need. He was unlearning his father's lessons of uninvolved aloofness. He was finding that passion and genuineness were very much intertwined; genuineness expressed from a passionate core.

Jordan walked into N & K's dressed appropriately from his run. His running clothes chosen depending on the weather, shorts and T-shirt for warmer days or close-fitting sweats and long-sleeved shirts for cooler ones. Before joining Micah, he stopped by Mr. Rothman's booth to say hello.

"Good run today?" asked Micah.

"Same as always, although a little slower." The morning was warmer than usual for late autumn and Micah, clad in green shorts and orange mesh T-shirt, was cooling down. His breathing slow and even and his stubbled face flush with redness around his neck with a sheen of perspiration on his cheeks.

"You are such a good runner. Why haven't you entered any races?"

"I don't want to be professional," quipped Jordan.

"Professional? Most runners are amateurs, aren't they?"

"Well, yes, but I don't want to run for someone else's approval or for trophies or ribbons. That's what I mean by 'professional.' I run for me and my own satisfaction. My father always told me to 'run like the wind inside you and not the one behind or in front of you.' I've never been a competitive sort. The high school track coach was always trying to get me to join the track team. I always declined by telling him I wanted to be the wind, not controlled by it. I think that's what my father was trying to teach me and I suppose it was my way of explaining why I didn't want to run competitively. I'm pretty sure the track coach didn't understand."

Micah took a sip of coffee, set down his mug and said, "I get it. I'm trying to find 'the wind' inside my character."

Portia approached with a mug and pot of coffee, pouring coffee for Jordan, and asking him and Micah for their orders. Micah surprised both Jordan and Portia by asking for a bowl of oatmeal with raisins, brown sugar, and a touch of low-fat milk. "I'm on a personal reclamation project and trying to eat healthier," said Micah with a twist of humor in his voice.

Portia wrote his order on her pad and remarked, "We are always here to help our regular customers."

Al, who was just leaving, paused next to Portia and quipped, "We're always trying to be regular," before walking away with a smile as he doffed his fedora towards Portia's husband who was clearing dishes from the counter. Mort followed Al, stopped next to Portia, thanked her for her service, and said in a low voice directed toward Jordan, "One of these days, my dear friend Al will find the time to be a little more appropriate and then the world will have turned itself on end."

Portia remarked, "Mort must be the most thankful person alive. There will be another thank-you note for me on the table along with a generous tip. What will you have, Jordan?"

Jordan looked up at Portia and said, "I'll support my friend Micah and have the same." Portia walked away and Jordan said to Micah, "He changed my life."

"Who? Al?"

"No, Mr. Rothman. He changed my life by being true to himself. Most of his students didn't appreciate him, but I did. I do."

Micah was not sure what had happened. Jordan was a no-show for their next breakfast. He sat wondering if he had the wrong date. He had been so engrossed on finishing the new draft of *The Hero Within* and had been prone to confusing dates and times. He had recently missed a dentist appointment and arrived for haircut two hours early. He repeatedly promised himself to learn how to use the calendar application on his cell phone. Portia asked if he wanted to order breakfast while waiting, but he said he'd continue to nurse his coffee for a while longer.

Micah sipped coffee and thumbed through the latest draft when a gentleman who looked like he could be Jordan's older brother entered N & K's. He approached Micah's booth holding a rectangular wooden box and asked, "Are you Micah the writer?"

Micah immediately realized this athletic-looking man was Jordan's father and sensed something was not right. He felt a chill at the base of his neck and a nervous twitch in his stomach. "Yes, I am. You must be Jordan's dad. He looks exactly like you."

"I am. He told me he often met you here for breakfast after the incident when you came to his aid. Unfortunately, I have some tough news. Jordan was struck by a car a few weeks ago while he was on his morning run. He was taken to the hospital but died from complications due to internal injuries three days later." Jordan's father's eyes pooled with tears and his voice quivered. "Before he passed, he was able to tell us how much he loved us and also make one request."

Micah's face paled with the news and his eyes also teared. "I'm so sorry. Your son had become a good friend over the past year. I enjoyed his company and conversation."

"He felt the same about you, too. He told his mother and me about the book you were writing and how it once had his name in the title. He wanted you to have what's in this box and also asked that you pass along one of his unique fountain pens to Mr. Rothman."

Micah took the pen box from Jordan's father. The walnut-colored box was burnished to a high gloss and etched into the hinged lid was the word Pens. Micah lifted the lid to reveal six pens filling slots lined with green felt.

"Those are six pens Jordan restored and kept for his own use. They were very special to him. This orange pen," said Jordan's father pointing with a shaky finger to an antique, orange Waterman, "is a pen he wanted you to give to Mr. Rothman. He said that he would understand its meaning. The others he wanted you to have."

Micah looked carefully at the collection. He picked out an older dark blue Conklin Duragraph and thought about the pride and hard work Jordan put into his love of pens. He recalled how Jordan shared that Mr. Rothman had changed his life. It wasn't merely about him introducing him to fountain pens. It was more about what those pens symbolized: quiet style, historical connections, the importance of caring for valued items, and the freedom to be expressive in an artful way. Mr. Rothman was the one teacher who wrote thank-you notes to express gratitude, which, for Jordan, proved that the pen was mighty when used for a kind purpose.

"Mr. Rothman eats breakfast here every morning but he has already left. I'll make a point to come by early tomorrow and pass along the sad news as well as this pen."

Micah walked into N & K's just after it opened. He was slumped a little more than usual. The morning was foggy, which cast a chilly and fitting gloom for the task before him. Seated at the last booth and facing the door was Mort. Al had yet to arrive and Mort was busy writing a note and taking small sips of coffee. He looked up as Micah approached and slid into the vinyl seat across from him.

"Mort, I'm Micah. We have a mutual connection in Jordan."

"Yes, I know who you are. Funny we've never spoken before. Jordan told me about the kindness you showed him when you found him hurt and in pain in the park. That was over a year ago, I believe. I wrote you a thank-you note after that happened."

"I'm sorry. I never received it. I would have said something," replied Micah.

"Oh, I don't actually send them anymore. It's more of a personal exercise. It's a bit like morning meditation for me, a regular chance to practice gratitude."

"I know what you mean. I meditate at The Pond almost every day. It's my way of trying to quiet my mind. I think this may be something else we have in common. Unfortunately, I have some terrible news to share with you. Yesterday, Jordan's father informed me that Jordan has died." Micah continued to fill in Mort about Jordan's demise, as Mort sat mouth agape in disbelief, bent forward with his chest pressed against the tabletop.

Micah removed the orange fountain pen from his sweatshirt's pocket and handed it to Mort. "Before he died, Jordan told his parents that he wanted you to have this pen. He said you'd understand."

Portia came over to the booth with a pot of coffee and a white ceramic mug and noticed the pen that Micah had just handed Mort. Mort shared what Micah had just told him.

"Oh, my gosh, do you think Jordan was the mystery note writer, Mort?"

Mort removed the pen's cap, took out a fresh note card from his pocket, and scribbled a few orange-colored lines before staring at Portia with astonishment just as Al pushed open the front door, doffed his hat towards Portia's husband who was busy preparing an order, and loudly proclaimed, "Here today, will be here tomorrow, and the day after that at my favorite food establishment," drawing perplexed attention from several non-regulars sitting at the counter and at a booth at the other end of the restaurant. Others who regularly experienced Al's flamboyance ignored him. He strode with attention-getting presence to his regular booth to sit with his best friend and noticed Micah, to whom he had not been introduced.

Mort invited Micah to slide over and make room for Al. "This is Micah, the author Jordan told us about. He just shared with me some very sad news." Mort became quiet and unable to tell Al what Micah had just reported. He sat stunned, listening to the kitchen's industrial exhaust fan. Al knew after forty years of friendship when to be silent and give Mort space and time to process. Portia poured coffee for Micah, refilled Mort's mug, and retrieved a mug for Al before repeating to Al what Mort had just learned about Jordan.

Micah and Al took sips of coffee while Mort sat quietly, eyes cast downward, his right thumb rubbing nervously into his left palm. Portia slid into Mort's side of the booth, put her arm around his shoulder and pulled him close. She whispered into his ear causing him to nod his head and smile.

"You are so wise, Portia," said Mort with an even voice. "Jordan did write those thank you notes. He changed me more than he could have ever imagined."

Lucy Stories

The Big Lie

Whenever he thought of vegans, he imagined the limitations of narrowness. He believed anyone who practiced a restrictive diet...vegan, fruitarian, basic vegetarian, ketogenetic, paleo, South Beach, Atkins, pescatarian... was a nut case. He thought of animals like aardvarks as one-dimensional with a diet of ants and termites. He thought of bears who ate a lot of berries and an occasional fish as living meaningless lives. He believed that what separated humans from the rest of the animal kingdom were their omnivorous diets. He dismissed imagination as something that made humans different from other animals. He would respond to those who used that as an argument with, "All life has imagination, but all life doesn't savor what it eats." He believed that to enjoy life one must keep all dietary options on the table. After all, he would tell friends, "Our teeth are designed to eat everything, to enjoy tastes, textures and variety." When his opinion was challenged, he'd shake his head and suggest the challenger had yet to evolve. He believed there were two kinds of people: evolved and not evolved.

Stan, as he was known through deception, was a forty-four-year-old owner of fifty-one successful burger joints that offered a precise menu of three burger choices: plain, cheese, or chili; fries or onion rings; milkshakes; cola, root beer, lemon-lime soda, and free water with a 25-cent cup charge. Each restaurant had a drive-up window, ten tables for inside dining, and ten tables for outside dining. His employees were paid minimum wage but, remarkably, he offered fully paid medical plans for his fulltime employees; however, each fast-food restaurant employed only two fulltime employees: one restaurant manager and one fulltime cook. What made his establishments successful were fresh, locally sourced ingredients, including hamburger buns made by a local bakery, and a certain attitude by his employees of what Stan called "East Coast bully." Customers seemed to enjoy the clipped banter they experienced from adolescents who never said "Mr., Mrs. or Ms." when "bud, gal, dude, or chick" would do. Stan was proud of his training program that used a professional actor to teach high school kids how to be "disrespectful with charm."

Each month a sign, which appeared to be hand lettered, was hung in his restaurants to demonstrate what he called his "keen sense of practical humor without being a practical joke" with total disregard for who might or might not be offended. Some examples included:

- One hamburger shows restraint. Two or more show your belly.
- No shoes, no service. No clothes, free fries.
- Opinions and condiments are free.
- Keep pets outside and children leashed inside.
- We have 29 flavors of milkshakes that come in chocolate, vanilla, or strawberry.
- Special orders gladly taken but never delivered.
- The complaint department is just down the road over the abyss.

None of Stan's employees had ever met him. Stan never visited any of his establishments, as he had a small team to whom he referred as quality control infiltrators overseeing day-to-day operations. Even they had never met Stan. All communications were by email or phone and mostly through the corporate office, which was staffed by an attorney and small team of accountants. They, too, were insulated from Stan, whom they referred to as a mystery entrepreneur.

In fact, Stan had two personas. There was the public image he projected as Stan the purveyor of high-quality fast foods with a generous helping of outlandish opinions and insolent behavior. And, while he did find fad dieters to be unevolved, the opinionated Stan never ate burgers, fries, onion rings, or sodas. He thought ground beef to be below his station in life, found fries and onion rings to be proletarian, and drank only fine wine, good whiskey, or filtered water. Stan was a prep school and Ivy League educated child of privilege with an undergraduate degree in philosophy and post-graduate MBA and law degrees, all with honors. He passed the bar exam on his first try but never practiced law. He thought about politics for a nanosecond. It was when he was dating Melissa, who ate only fast foods, that he decided to start a business based on simplicity, obfuscation, and human frailty. Somehow, most of his relationships with women were based on simplicity, obfuscation, and frailty.

Stan was his assumed identity. He took every precaution to keep his false identity separate from his real one. His real name was Bernard "Bernie" Levinson. He lived life as a strict routine, with little time for activities that didn't feed his narcissism or wallet. Every morning at 5:00 a.m. in his fully equipped basement gym he put his wiry, five-foot six-inch body through a strenuous one-hour workout designed and encouraged by his personal trainer Bridget…every morning, seven days a week, 365 days a year. Bridget had the weekends off and her husband Brad worked the weekends. Bridget and Brad had no clue to Bernie's alternate identity. Bernie was determined to not become the obese and flatulent version of his father, who ate well and far too much.

On Monday mornings at precisely 9:00 a.m., Bernie met with his two-person publicity and legal team in his home office where they produced a weekly Stan's Burgers video clip that was posted on social media and selected television spots. The two-person team were the only ones to know Bernie personally. They were sworn to secrecy, having signed a lengthy non-disclosure agreement and a lucrative contract that most folks in their position would only dream of. They were the ones who controlled all operations, including all communications to and from the quality control infiltrators. Bernie had constructed a simple, yet effective, structure that kept him in control and his true identity unknown.

However, Bernie still found a way to be in the limelight. During those Monday morning sessions with his publicity and legal team, Bernie would don his Stan disguise: huge Poncho Villa mustache, heavy Mr. Magoo glasses, fake nose prosthesis…which he didn't bother to use makeup to blend the seam with his skin…, a bright red Stan's baseball cap, a set of upper dentures that fit over his own perfect teeth and gave the illusion of a large gap between two buck teeth, and an obnoxious Bronx accent. At least, Bernie thought it was a Bronx accent although his team described it as an English-gone-cockney-got-lost-somewhere-on the East Coast abomination. Stan had become something of a perfect anti-celebrity celebrity.

After assuming his Stan identity, he would be videotaped while improvising a short, fifteen to thirty second, Stan's Burger advertisement. Bernie had been influenced by other loudmouth television hucksters who used style over substance to influence their followers. Stan had followers: over three million on Instagram and Twitter, and tens of thousands of likes on Facebook. Bernie had no followers or likes because Bernie had no social media accounts. He thought social media was nothing more than a vehicle for scam and deceit and he was more than happy to take advantage.

Bernie usually completed the taping in two or three takes. He would take a deep breath and break into Stan saying, "This is Stan of Stan's Burgers, the restaurant where any decision you make is a good one regardless of the consequences. We've got burgers and shakes and sodas and free water. And we've got a monthly slogan to help you with the results of your decision. This month it's 'Take a break at Stan's Burgers. You need the fat and I need the money.' Remember, at Stan's Burgers you'll get food cooked the way I think it should be cooked and sass from one of our disrespectful servers. See you at Stan's Burgers, the most loved fast food on the planet."

Yet, there was another secret that Bernie kept from his Stan's Burger team of confidants. He owned a fine dining restaurant in a neighboring town. BL's was a high-end steakhouse where a bottle of wine cost as much as a pair of expensive women's designer shoes and the steaks were aged for a minimum of three months. It was Bernie's only investment that did not turn a profit and barely broke even. He paid the restaurant manager an elaborate sum to maintain the highest quality, which included wages above industry standards for all employees. A fulltime sommelier maintained a prize-winning wine collection. He employed a certified whiskey master to maintain a stock of the finest whiskeys from around the world. Reservations were mandatory and a dress code required coat and tie for gentleman. Bernie made no dress requirement for ladies, as he believed women always knew how to dress appropriately.

The restaurant was designed with understated elegance. Tables were set with crisp white tablecloths and napkins, which were folded in rectangles and placed next to silver flatware that didn't call attention to itself. Booths, featuring deep maroon leather, and tables were arranged to maximize privacy. The lighting allowed for easy reading of menus but enough intimacy to encourage low-voiced conversation. Other than a few large pieces of abstract art from Bernie's personal collection, the walls were a light cream. Bernie's personal booth was in a far corner and the only one always set for four persons, although Bernie frequently dined alone. On those nights he enjoyed dinner alone, he was called Mr. Bernard. On those nights he had a date or other guests, he was Mr. Levinson. It was on a date when Bernie's world changed.

Bernie met Lucy at the Saturday farmer's market on a warm, fall day. He spotted her while she was looking over a selection of baked goods at Marcel's Patisserie booth trying to decide between an almond croissant or an apricot tart when Bernie approached and asked, "If I purchase one of each, will you join me for coffee at the picnic bench?"

Before asking, Bernie checked her hands for rings or any other overt sign of marriage or other commitment. Lucy was wearing a dark blue knit top, tan slacks, and pink tennis shoes. Her long black hair and caramel complexion reminded Bernie of a beautiful Brazilian woman.

"My name is Bernie and I'm not usually so forward," he said with a little less confidence than when he first approached Lucy. "May I buy you a coffee?"

Lucy knew she was a beautiful woman and was used to impulsive come-ons. However, when she turned and looked at Bernie, she saw a kindness in his blue eyes and some comedy in his huge floppy sun hat.

She smiled and asked, "What kind of coffee?"

"If you don't mind me saying, you look South American, and they have a very nice Brazilian coffee at the booth across the way."

Lucy laughed. "What is it about men who think dark-skinned women are from some exotic country. And, if that's part of your pick-up line, start searching for a new one. I'm Israeli. And, no, I'm not related to Gal Gadot. But, because you look harmless, I'll be happy to sit and have coffee with you."

They both ordered macchiatos and shared the apricot tart that Bernie purchased. They sat quietly across from one another for a few minutes before Lucy asked with a directness that Bernie would find to be an endearing quality, "What do you do when you're not buying pastries and trying to pick up women?"

"I own a restaurant, BL's, you might know about."

"That's a fancy place. A little too rich for my taste," said Lucy.

"What is your taste?"

"I'm more of a simple hamburger gal."

"And one who enjoys good baked goods and fancy coffee," said Bernie with a touch of irony in his tone.

"Well, yes, there's that. My likes and dislikes are not always predictable. You might find me to be full of surprises."

Bernie stared at Lucy and her flawless complexion, peered into her dark eyes, and asked, "Would you like to have dinner with me at my restaurant tonight?"

Bernie, dressed in his newest and darkest black suit, bright yellow silk tie, yellow socks, and mirror-polished black Oxfords, knocked on Lucy's front door. Her house was a modest, mid-Century house in a child-friendly neighborhood. Her front lawn recently mowed and flower beds with an abundance of rose bushes. Lucy opened her door wearing freshly ironed jeans, scooped neck white T-shirt, and a red cotton blazer.

"Bernie, do I need to change?"

"No, you look perfect."

Bernie was driving his Audi A8 and opened the passenger door and Lucy thanked him for being such a perfect gentleman. When they arrived at BL's, the valet opened the door for Lucy and greeted Bernie with a swift salute and said, "Good to see you, Mr. Levinson. Enjoy your dinner."

"Mr. Levinson? You're a Mr. Levinson!" exclaimed Lucy. "You really do own this place."

"It's one of my pleasures and I hope yours, too."

After being greeted by the maître d', Bernie led Lucy to his booth. "Would you like a cocktail or something else before dinner?"

"Although my tastes are probably not as rich as this restaurant, I do enjoy a good red wine."

Bernie instructed the sommelier to decant one of his rarer Cabernets, which he knew to be in the $500 range and also bring a selection of cheeses for them to enjoy before ordering dinner. Lucy looked around the restaurant before nodding at a painting on the wall across from their booth.

"That's a beautiful painting. It looks like a de Kooning."

"It is."

"An original?"

"So, I'm told."

"Wow! This restaurant must do really well."

"I have other investments."

The wine was served along with an aged sharp cheddar, richly veined gorgonzola, and thinly sliced rounds of fresh baguette. They both took their time savoring the wine and cheese. Bernie watched Lucy sample her wine like someone who had experience with tasting fine wine. She held the wineglass by its stem, swished the wine while observing how it clung to the inside of the glass, and inhaled its bouquet before taking a sip and allowing it to linger in her mouth before swallowing.

"You have some experience with enjoying good wine," he commented.

"Yes, I've always enjoyed wine but have never tasted anything as good as this before."

Dinner followed and Bernie was surprised when Lucy ordered a filet. BL's did offer a gourmet burger and, since Lucy had mentioned she was a 'burger kind of gal', he thought that's what she'd order.

"I'm surprised you didn't order the burger."

"Well, I do like a cheap burger now and then but tonight seems special and the wine set a mood for steak. Besides, there's nothing cheap about a $30 burger on this menu."

"I'm really not much for cheap," replied Bernie with all the sincerity his version of Bernie could muster.

Bernie walked Lucy to her front door where they lingered for a moment. Lucy leaned forward and kissed Bernie on his cheek while giving him a loose hug. Bernie asked if there would be a second date and Lucy agreed to another dinner. "But it has to be a place of my choosing."

Bernie drove off wondering who Lucy really was. Was she a burger or a steak gal? Beer or fine wine? Was there a fancy dresser under her blazer and denim look? What was her real self? Their dinner conversation was pleasant and typically shallow first date fare. She learned about his growing up as a child of privilege and elite schooling. He learned of her hard-working parents, a brother and sister with whom she was close, and her family's traditional holiday celebrations.

"I went to public schools, a good state college and I am proud of the small insurance agency that I own with my sister. I'm also very proud of my brother who started and franchised a chain of boutique vitamin and nutritional supplement stores. You might say we've achieved a bit of the American Dream my parents sought when they came to this country from Eastern Europe. I really value the lessons my parents taught us. The importance of hard work and honesty. The need to be genuine and true to oneself. Don't you think that's what's really important?"

"I'm not sure I've ever thought about what 'oneself' means," opined Bernie. "It's possible that we could have more than one self. Maybe over time as we grow and mature; maybe even multiple selves at one time. I don't mean a Sybil kind of thing. Rather, a product of circumstances. I remember when I was a student that I was a very different person at school than I was at home. I think we behave differently depending on where we are and what role we need to play to succeed or even survive."

"Bernie, I'm not sure I get what you're saying. You've become a very successful restauranteur. Aren't you comfortable with that identity? Or do you have others you are not sharing?"

The conversation at dinner left Bernie feeling ambivalent. His hidden identity had never felt like much of a burden, but now he wasn't so sure. How could he reconcile his immediate feelings for Lucy with his own subterfuge? He could justify profit motive, but not deceit and blatant falsehoods. Had he created a wall of isolation from which he could never emerge?

A few days later, Bernie called and asked Lucy to dinner again, "As promised, you get to choose the restaurant."

"Oh, yes, I'll surprise you. No reservations will be necessary and be sure to dress casually."

As Bernie, casual dress meant khaki slacks, blue shirt, and tan Sperry Top-Siders. He also wore a red Stanley's Burger baseball cap thinking it would be a fun statement showing support for a cheap hamburger. For Lucy, it was the same dress as her first date without the blazer. Bernie drove up to Lucy's house in his black Miata, which he counted as his casual car. The sun was low in the sky, there was no wind and the temperature warm enough for the convertible top to be open. Bernie was surprised when Lucy walked down the front walk wearing a red Stan's Burger cap and a radiating smile.

"I guess we're going to Stan's," said Bernie.

"Yes, let's go to the original on Main Street. Believe it or not, my brother worked there when he was in high school. It's a good thing we're going after the dinner rush, because they only have ten tables inside and outside."

"Really? How do they do so well?" Bernie didn't feel comfortable with being so blatantly untruthful with Lucy.

"From what I understand, this Stan character has found a way to charm folks with a cartoonish charm and faked reality. Nobody I know believes anything he says in those weird ads he runs in a totally fake disguise. Even though the ads sometime proclaim the food to be unhealthy, the burgers are especially good, and the shakes are made with real ice cream. It may be fast food and it may be unhealthy, but it's still good fast food. Indulging occasionally isn't all that bad. Besides, it's all about showmanship and tasty food, so who cares about the buffoonery."

Bernie sensed an opening and perhaps an opportunity to confess his multiple identities to Lucy. He was determined to find the right time. After parking the Miata around the corner from Stan's Burgers they walked to the outside window. Lucy suggested they eat outside since the weather was so nice and it was still light outside. They both ordered the special burger basket, which included a cheeseburger, fries, and choice of milkshake. They both ordered vanilla shakes.

They sat facing each other at the round table with attached seats that hung from the center support like four arms of an octopus. A large overhang provided shade while they waited for their order number to be called. Lucy continued her commentary about Stan's Burgers. Bernie was impressed with her knowledge and wondered why she seemed so fascinated with Stan's.

"When my brother was in high school and working at this very Stan's, he would come home and tell stories about how they were trained to be 'rude with a smile.' I thought that was hilarious until my brother decided to start his own business using a similar strategy. I was appalled. It went against everything our parents had taught us."

Bernie listened as Lucy, again, raised the question of family values. He thought about his own family and couldn't think of any life lessons passed along by either his mother or father. Dinnertime conversations, when they were infrequently at the same table, were mostly about family or acquaintances who were not as financially successful. They would talk about a poor uncle down on his luck or a needy cousin who they felt was unmotivated to do well. Almost all his interactions with his parents were transactional. He was paid for chores, good grades, successes in sports. Bernie was feeling a need to proclaim his own duplicity.

Without fanfare, a tall thirtysomething man set their orders on the table before them and sat down with an I-got-you grin. He wore a fake nose and Mr. Magoo glasses.

"Nice to see you, Stan. It's been a while."

"I don't know you and my name is Bernie," said with a touch incredulity. "What's with the Stan disguise. Yes, I've seen the character on T.V."

Lucy said, "Bernie or Stan or whoever you are, this is my brother. He worked at this very Stan's when he was in high school. He learned how to be rude and self-centered. Our family had a very rough time getting him back on track. A good part of that was finding out who Stan really was and the ruse you've pulled with phoniness and greed. He almost went down the wrong road. But now, the jig is up, so to speak. You have a choice: either tell the truth on your own or we'll do it for you."

Lucy's Big Lie

Lucy and her brother enjoyed their cheeseburgers, fries and vanilla shakes while seated at the table outside Stan's burgers. They abhorred Bernie Levinson and his fake Stan identity as much as they enjoyed his burger chain's food. After Lucy confronted Bernie with the choice that he either tell the truth about his fake persona or have it revealed by her, he calmly rose without a word and casually walked back to his Miata and slowly drove away. Lucy was taken aback by Bernie's lack of outrage, his bland affect. A few minutes later, she received a terse text message, "You'll hear from me later."

"He just walked out!" exclaimed Lucy.

Lucy's brother asked, "What do you think that means?'

"He'll probably threaten some sort of lawsuit. It's sad because I really think there's a vulnerability with Bernie that he's afraid to reveal." Lucy wanted to feel good about how she and her brother had surprised and threatened Bernie. However, she felt a sadness for her own behavior. When she confronted Bernie, she did it with a neutral posture and little emotion in her voice, maybe even a tinge of regret. She had persuaded her brother to abet in their own subterfuge forcing Bernie to publicly admit to his own underhanded ways. Had she compromised her own set of moral principles from the moment she drew his attention at an outdoor farmer's market? Afterward, she gleefully informed her brother that her fourth time at the market had worked to attract Bernie's attention while playing the role of a confused woman trying to decide on a baked item. Their plan to eventually confront Bernie had begun when she secured a date through her own deception. She and her brother believed that forcing Bernie to expose his own duplicity justified their strategy.

Lucy began to sense her own doubt after their date at his high-end restaurant. There was never any sign of his outrageously brash Stan alter ego, which encouraged his Stan's Burger teenage employees to behave with comic in-your-face disrespect. On the other hand, Bernie spoke with a pleasant and courteous demeaner. He treated his restaurant's staff with respect and no positional deference. It was clear that there was mutual respect between him and those in his employ. He exhibited class without presumption.

Lucy wondered if Bernie's false Stan identity was simply motivated by greed and symptomatic of his upbringing. Did he grow up in a family that valued falsehood and deception as acceptable behavior if it led to financial wealth? How could anyone consciously possess two opposing personalities and use them to manipulate others? Regardless of her thoughts, Lucy believed that she and her brother were right in demanding that Bernie come clean with his false identity. Afterall, they reasoned, when Lucy's brother worked at Stan's while in high school, he easily succumbed to the training that encouraged...really demanded from impressionable youth...impolite and in-your-face behavior, although with a wink and a smirk. They were motivated to stop what they believed were unhealthy emotional shenanigans.

Later that night, Lucy received a text message from Bernie inviting her to meet for dinner at his fancy and very expensive BL's restaurant. He promised a good meal and asked that she not bring her brother. He added, "No anger, just conversation."

Lucy immediately called her brother. "What do you think?"

"Don't go," said her brother without demand, but rather concern.

"Maybe he wants to talk about how he will disclose his two identities."

"Maybe. Maybe not."

Lucy arrived at BL's wearing a dark green dress, flowing white scarf, and carrying a simple black purse. She was not dressed as casually as she had been for their first date. She had decided before accepting Bernie's invitation that she would match his formality, which she considered a bit of a power play on her part. She had once read something about dressing for success and figured this was one of those opportunities. She was surprised when she was shown to Bernie's personal booth and saw that he was not wearing a tie or an expensive dark suit. He had on a blue Oxford shirt and, when he stood as she approached, she noticed pressed denim pants and black New Balance tennis shoes.

"Thanks for coming, Lucy. I was afraid you wouldn't show, and we do have something important to talk about."

"Is this a trick?" asked Lucy. "You've dressed down and now you seem unusually relaxed for someone being asked to reveal a closely-held secret."

"No, this is not a trick. This is how I'm most comfortable. I dress more formally because I think it's expected. Maybe I need to learn how to set my own expectations rather than have them controlled by others."

"That would be an interesting start," said Lucy without any hint of sarcasm. "I'm interested in hearing how you intend to respond to what my brother and I put before you. How are you intending to reveal the truth about your con job?"

Bernie listened with a controlled blankness, his shoulders relaxed and his expression showing no signs of anger or anxiousness. He had the perfectly assumed stoicism of a professional poker player.

"Well, I'd disagree with your characterization of Stan as being a 'con job.' I'd call it a smart marketing strategy. And I'd also take issue with you and your brother thinking I have multiple identities. I think I'm fairly secure in knowing who I am. I am not interested in exposing, as you would say, Stan's identity. It's an important part of my business and I'd like to keep it that way. So, I have a proposal." Bernie paused and tried looking at Lucy as a businessman opening the door to negotiations. As much as he tried to maintain professional decorum, he still had feelings for Lucy that he had never had with other women.

"Let's order dinner, Bernie. Then we'll talk. And, since I agreed to meet you at your fancy restaurant, I'm in the mood for a well-made dinner."

"Fair enough," said Bernie. "Will it be a steak or the gourmet hamburger?"

"Neither. I think a nice, chopped salad and what the menu refers to as the Frenchiest French onion soup."

Bernie laughed. "Oh, now you are playing the marketing game. We'd never say 'Frenchiest' at BL's. But the soup is really extraordinary. I think I'll have the same. Would you mind if I chose a good California Pinot Gris? It goes well with the soup."

While Bernie ordered their meals, Lucy looked at the de Kooning hanging on the wall across from their booth. It had caught her attention the first time they met for dinner, and she imagined that Bernie's appreciation for abstract expressionism was an apt description of his own lifestyle. Then, again, he might only appreciate the form for its monetary value and not its unique style. She interpreted the painted bursts of colors and skewed shapes as representative of Bernie's grotesque version of Stan's outsized and deliberately impolite personality.

Lucy's spell with de Kooning was broken when Bernie said, "I have a proposition for you to consider."

"Do you?"

"I do. And I hope you won't be offended by it. Please, listen to everything I have to say before you respond."

"I'll try."

Bernie lifted a plain, black leather portfolio from the booth's bench seat and placed it on the table. "My attorney has prepared a contract that

I hope you'll find agreeable. I don't expect you to sign it tonight because I know you'll want to talk it over with your brother before deciding. First, allow me to tell you what the gist of it is."

Lucy expected this sort of play by Bernie, and she tried to remain placid as Bernie went on to outline his proposal. She kept telling herself that this meeting was nothing more than a client session at her office, where meeting with her clients about their insurance policies could sometimes be tense.

Bernie began by explaining how hurt he felt when Lucy and her brother confronted him. He said that he was uncomfortable with conflict and didn't know how to respond in the moment, so he just walked away. He shared his own discomfort with not being fully open with Lucy on their first date. He expressed that he had feelings for her.

"What I'm proposing is a series of contributions to whatever charity you'd prefer. In exchange, you will agree to have five dinners with me at any restaurant you choose. However, I'll only agree to go to Stan's Burgers for the fifth dinner. At that dinner, we'll determine, if it's still necessary, who will reveal Stan's true identity."

The salad course arrived as Bernie finished with his proposal. Lucy wasn't sure if she should laugh or shout. Instead, she asked with a hint of cynicism, "Are you trying to buy me off? You offer to donate $50,000 for each dinner date...that's a quarter of a million dollars...to have dinner with me and try to convince me to hide your ugly identity. What do you take me for? You say you have feelings. Well, you can't buy my feelings."

"I know what I'm suggesting seems presumptuous and maybe even demeaning to you. All I'm asking is for you to give me a chance. I want you to know the real me and, in the end, you decide the outcome."

"It's much more than a suggestion. I suggest we finish dinner and then I'll leave and get back to you in a few days."

They ate the remainder of their salad and soup in silence. Bernie kept his eyes on Lucy, which she found discomforting. Bernie's look was more than a stare; it was a plea. Lucy thought the soup to be the best French onion soup she had ever had. It was the 'Frenchiest' and the wine was a perfect pairing. She was determined not to compliment Bernie on the meal as she quietly stewed over his proposal.

When she stood to leave, Bernie said, "I owe you an apology. I thought my offer would give us a chance to know each other on better terms and also do some good. But you are correct, I'm merely trying to buy something that should not be for sale. Perhaps, I should just simply do as you and your brother insist I ought to do."

Lucy responded, "It was the 'Frenchiest' soup I've ever had. I'll get back to you in a few days."

A few days turned into a few weeks. Bernie wondered if Lucy had decided to drop the issue. He didn't know that Lucy and her brother were disagreeing about how to proceed. When Lucy shared Bernie's offer to her brother, she angrily suggested they tear it up and follow through with contacting the local media and telling the truth about Bernie and his false Stan identity.

Lucy's brother said, "As much as I despise the objectionable behaviors I was taught while working at Stan's Burgers, I'm not so sure it's any worse than the multitude of deceptive practices that already exist. Maybe we are being overly earnest about this. Maybe we've lost our sense of humor over what is clearly over-the-top marketing. Maybe we ought to try a different approach with Bernie."

"What are you suggesting?" asked Lucy.

"Perhaps, we've already done what we needed to do. I'm suggesting we do nothing."

Lucy's shoulders sagged in defeat. She told her brother that it was a lousy idea. She walked out of the room determined to take the issue to the next step. The next day she dropped in on the local newspaper's office and asked to speak with the editor. After explaining the purpose of her visit as being "important to maintaining community standards by exposing unscrupulous business practices," she was escorted to the city editor's office. She sat in a stiff-backed chair facing a gray, steel desk which held three computer screens, what appeared to be a variety of cell phones or possibly electronic notebooks, a black, leatherbound notebook, and a few standard issue pens and pencils. Hanging on the wall behind the desk was a sign proclaiming, "The facts, nothing but the facts, and a creative story."

A short, bony man strode in with the gait of a hungry greyhound, directed Lucy to stay seated, moved behind his desk and sat in an armless secretary's chair. He picked up a pencil, opened his notebook, and said, "I'm Mike Dillahunt and I understand you have an important story for us to tell."

"I do, but first I'm curious about the meaning of that sign behind you."

"Oh, an old friend gave that to me as a joke. He likes teasing me about so-called fake news and journalistic integrity. So, what piece of important news do we need to know."

Lucy took her time describing Bernie Levinson's unethical business practice of his invented Stan character, his encouragement of disrespectful behavior by impressionable adolescent employees, and his total disregard for truth in advertising. She finished by telling how Bernie was trying to extort her silence.

Mike Dillahunt listened while turning the pencil between his thumb and forefinger and never writing anything in his notebook. He stared at Lucy with the look of an elementary school teacher listening to a third grader complaining about a boy who yanked her ponytail at recess. After Lucy finished, he said, "Thank you for coming in. We will take your story under advisement." He stood and gestured towards his office door.

"Have a nice day."

Lucy left the newspaper office feeling humiliated and questioning herself. Clearly, Mike Dillahunt wasn't going to do anything. He probably thought she was something of a fringe element seeking attention over a trivial matter. Was she making her issue larger than it warranted? Was she being overly self-righteous? Was her brother's advice to do nothing the right choice?

Lucy used her cell phone to call Bernie. He answered on the first ring, and she said, "I'll have dinner with you tonight at BL's."

Bernie stood as Lucy approached his booth with less assuredness than before. Bernie noticed that she did not make eye contact until seated across from him, when she looked up and said, "I have something of a confession to make."

Before she could say anything more, Bernie asked her to pause and said, "We both do."

Lucy looked questioningly at Bernie raising her eyebrows and asked, "What do you mean?"

"Well, when you and your brother threatened to expose me, I allowed you to think that you had some power or leverage over me. And then I used that misperception to try and bargain you into a relationship. The contract that I said was drawn up by my attorney was also a ruse. It would seem that I'm skilled at being disingenuous, and for that I apologize. The reality is that I had already planned to unmask my Stan invention some time ago. Mike Dillahunt called me immediately after you left his office and that pushed the timeline forward. We've been friends for many years, and he was already aware of our upcoming promotion where I make a huge production of unmasking phony Stan, appear as myself, and announce new, courteous service at all Stan's Burgers along with an upgraded menu featuring plant-based additions to the menu. I have also established a Stan's Burger Foundation for Truth in Advertising. Your threat was an empty one, and I used it to try and manipulate you. I hope you'll forgive me."

"Forgive you?" blurted Lucy with a quiver in her voice as she inched out of the booth, stood, turned her back to Bernie and walked away.

Lucy Meets a Kind Man

He thought of himself as a kind man. Those who knew him thought of him as a kind man, too. He never intentionally drew attention to himself. At social engagements, he was not a mixer but would likely be found bent over in quiet conversation with one person for the entire time. It was only his size that caused him any undue attention. He stood six foot eight, straight as a two by four after many years of slumped over posture, with an explosion of curly red hair and pale skin subtly dotted with translucent freckles. He looked like a clown searching for his clown car.

Retired after an almost thirty-five-year career as a postman, he lives comfortably on his pension and a significant inheritance from an aunt who died peacefully with over five million dollars in a savings account and half a million in cash, which was discovered in neatly stacked baggies in her basement freezer. He had no other living relatives and hardly knew his aunt who left him all her worldly possessions with a short note that read: "To my tall nephew and son of my dear sister, I leave you my entire estate with the wish that you will spend it well." No one, not even her attorney, could explain such an extravagant estate. Her attorney knew that she lived frugally after her husband, who was significantly older, died after a short career as a stockbroker. The attorney surmised that sound investments had been made, but he could not explain the piles of freezer cash.

He had met his aunt a few times as a child and again as a young man before his parents were killed while attempting a tandem parasailing flight gone tragically wrong when they flew into a pair of high-voltage power lines. Orphaned at twenty-five, he delivered mail and spent his non-working time grieving inside his one-bedroom, rent-controlled apartment for five years. He emerged from his self-imposed isolation after he received word from his aunt's attorney of her passing along with notice of her funeral and his inheritance. He remembered his aunt as a very short, bosomy woman almost as round as she was tall. She was a hugger who didn't let go. The few times they met, he would peel himself away while the hot flush of embarrassment filled his cheeks. His mother was the exact opposite of her sister, tall and willowy with an aversion for closeness. He thought his mother and aunt must have been adopted by his grandparents with a dash of familial humor. He wished he had known his maternal grandparents.

For the next twenty years, he continued to deliver mail, spent little of his fortune, but no longer lived a loner's existence. Where he had walked with a pronounced stoop since becoming a towering figure in high school, he unfolded into a proud and confident stature while maintaining his reserved demeanor. With his newfound linearity came an awakening, a coming out of his social shyness. He began to engage with those at work and soon formed a couple of friendships, which resulted in regular stops at the local pub for an afterwork cocktail and often dinner. He began reading in earnest and joined a mystery book group recommended by his local library. He took golf lessons but abandoned all hope of ever breaking 100 and subsequently played without keeping score. Most surprisingly, women were attracted to him.

Especially tall women. Elegant women. Beautiful women with an agenda, some without. Women who were self-professed feminists and women who professed little. His height and soft-spoken kindness were magnetic. He might be shopping at the local grocery store searching for the perfect bunch of radishes when a woman would suddenly appear at his side looking up and asking if she could help. After examining and choosing an excellent cluster of rainbow radishes for him, she would ask with a flirtatious smile, "Are you thinking of a salad for one or perhaps two?" Another time, while trying to choose between a wild salmon filet or halibut cheeks, he was approached by a dark-haired woman wearing a red T-shirt, white shorts and flip-flops who said, "Pick the salmon and I'll make you a meal worthy of a four-star restaurant."

Whether salad or fish, meals often led to more meals and temporary relationships. His friends from work asked when he might settle down. He gained a reputation as one practicing serial monogamy. His male friends joked that he was living out their fantasies; his women friends shook their heads and told him to get serious. He wanted to get serious when he met Lucy.

They didn't meet while grocery shopping. And they didn't meet as a result of her making the first move. In fact, much to his regret, no first moves were made. They met after ordering meals at Stan's Burgers and finding only one available table outside.

He asked, "Do you mind if we share this table?"

"Of course not. It's just Stan's," replied Lucy.

They ate in silence for a few moments before Lucy remarked that she had once abhorred Bernie Levinson, the owner of Stan's Burgers. "I thought he was a despicable person, a deceiver and a phony, but then he had some sort of revelation and became even more of a folk hero. I suppose I've forgiven him for those misdeeds."

"You mean when he came clean about his invented Stan persona and dedicated his life to making Stan's a friendly place, other than the faked disrespect his employees were once known for. And now his foundation has become known for its charitable work. He's had several tributes written about him by the local press."

"Yeah, that Stan. Well, really Bernie. At least the burgers are good."

"It sounds like you might have a history with him."

"Let's just say it didn't go well."

They continued to munch on their burgers, fries, and shakes. He couldn't help noticing her dark beauty and the differences in their dining style. Lucy managed to slowly eat her burger without so much as a single drip while he hunched over his serving tray leaving a puddle of Stan's secret sauce which had dripped off his chin. He was also aware that she feigned any interest in him, while he closely observed her dark hair cut short and worn in a carefree manner, smooth bronze complexion, and brown eyes which expressed a mysterious sadness. He searched inwardly for the right words to begin a conversation but couldn't find any. He felt like a young teen at his first dance wanting to cross the gym floor and ask that cute girl for a dance, but only fast songs were being played and he didn't want to make a fool of himself.

After finishing half of her burger and hardly any of her fries, Lucy took a final sip of her barely touched vanilla shake, stood, and without saying anything, turned and walked away. It was the first time in a very long time that he had not drawn attention from a beautiful woman. The inflated sense of self that came after his emergence from his hermit-like existence took a blow. He felt like the proverbial fisherman who laments about the big one that got away.

He told his closest friends Goldie and Shel about his chance encounter with Lucy. After his aunt had died, they were ones he turned to for comfort. It was at Goldie's urging that he began to come out of his shell. Goldie was the taller of the two; she towered over her husband Shel by over half a foot. Several months after his aunt's passing, Goldie knocked on his door and, without saying a word, walked into his unkept apartment and began cleaning and straightening out furniture and accessories. She even sorted through his limited wardrobe, grouping pants, shirts, sweaters, and other items into what she called "appropriate fashion statements for someone without an eye for any style." She moved her long, trim body with a ballerina's grace and efficiency. After putting the finishing touches on the kitchen including a complete rearrangement of his cupboards into "groupings that make sense", she turned to him and said, "Grieving will continue and so must your life. Shel and I will be over later to take you out to dinner. We'll talk then."

At dinner, she spoke while Shel sat quietly enjoying his spaghetti and meatballs. He sipped chianti and listened. "You need other friends besides us. You're a good-looking man with a good job and virtually no pressing responsibilities. It's time to get some important responsibilities. Most of all, you are a kind man. So, get out there and be kind. And stop slouching. I like the idea of looking up at a man for a change," she said with a loving glance at her short and burly husband Shel. Goldie's prodding along with Shel's nodding in agreement had its desired effect.

Now, they listened without interjecting any comment or judgment as they always did when he talked about his encounters with women. However, when he mentioned his attraction to Lucy without her showing any interest along with her abrupt departure, Shel said, "You can't win them all." And Goldie admonished, "You think you're such a big shot. You're just a tall man with a short ego."

"And you, Goldie, are my most profound friend," he said with a genuinely warm smile.

He decided, after a serendipitous encounter while taking a walk by a local schoolyard, that he would try basketball, again. All through high school despite the fact that his gangly build appeared to move in multiple, opposing directions as he walked through the school's hallways, coaches tried unsuccessfully to persuade him to join the team. Coaches knew they couldn't coach height, but they could coach it to get in the way of opposing jump shots. He attended one practice and left midway after enduring jibes from the other players and a coach who was exasperated by each one of his missteps and inability to follow directions.

Why try again after never having tried any other sport except for a stab at golf and his subsequent scorecard-free rounds? It's when he found himself one Saturday walking by a nearby schoolyard where a group of over-the-hill men were playing half-court basketball with lots of trash talk and loud bravado. One of the graying geezers called out, “Hey, tall guy, we could use a little help over here. How about it?” Wearing a loose, short-sleeved shirt buttoned to the neck, Levi’s, and tasseled loafers, he found he could stand near the basket, receive a pass lofted to him while the short players, who had no jump left in their tired old legs, watched as he banked the ball off the backstop for an easy score. The next time he showed up, he wore a T-shirt, Bermuda shorts, and brand-new bright orange Converse high top tennis shoes, an outfit not coordinated by Goldie. He began playing every week and found comfort in being around a group of guys who used putdowns and profanity to build comradery. He was the only one who did not partake of the irreverent banter. Often his fellow teammates would yell, “Hey, Mr. Nice Guy, pass the fucking ball for a change.” They would play for an hour or until someone pulled up lame with a leg cramp, twisted ankle, lack of breath or other real or imagined malady as an excuse to get a beer or light meal.

It was while he and his fellow Rabbit Survivors, whom they had dubbed themselves in homage to a John Updike character, were enjoying pizza and beer when Lucy approached from behind, tapped his shoulder and asked, “Aren’t you the guy from Stan’s?”

He looked up at Lucy, smiled with recognition, and was about to respond when one of the Rabbit Survivors pointed at him and blurted, “You’re that guy!”

“Yes, I’m that guy. And you’re that gal. I’m Simon. I don’t believe I know your name.”

“I’m Lucy.”

“Nice to see you again, Lucy. Do you dance?’

The Mime and the Elf

Outside the shopping mall entrance stood a bell ringer decked out in her finest elf costume. For the most part, passersby ignored her enthusiastic holiday greeting by looking straight ahead with insincere purpose. However, that all changed when, on the other side of the automatic doors, a mime dressed in a red unitard and sporting a Santa beard and holiday hat arrived and began moving with a languid grace before a sign he had propped up against the wall that read "Thank you Santa from your Jewish friends."

Soon thereafter, the mall's assistant manager emerged and turned menacingly toward the mime. "You are not authorized to be here. You need to vacate the premises immediately," said the officious assistant manager with all the bluster he could summon from his ill-filling suit and Christmas tree tie.

The elf interjected, "It's okay. He's with me and helping with our collections."

The mime continued with his interpretative dance, which, if anyone should be asked, would have difficulty explaining. The mime appeared to be performing something akin to a slow-motion version of the Mouse King from The Nutcracker Ballet only in a very small and defined space. At least, that's what was suggested by the music coming out of a miniature speaker attached to a smart phone which the mime had placed next to the thank-you sign.

"The permit allows for only one bell ringer. I'm afraid he needs to leave before I call security."

With the manager's second demand, the mime paused with his body straight, feet pointed in opposite directions, arms also held straight with hands pointed outwardly like his feet, and an exaggerated frown shown through his fluffy white beard.

The elf pled, "It's rare, maybe never, when a Jew has helped with our cause. Please, let him be here as part of my permit."

The mime raised his arms, cocked his head to one side, and placed is hands beneath his chin in his own quiet plea for mercy. The mime versus management standoff had attracted a small audience of onlookers who didn't know what to make of things. Someone called out, "This is no place for a Jew." Another crisply said, "That's not very Christian of you." The situation was getting tense. The first disparager retorted, "They killed Jesus and now he's mocking the elf."

The assistant manager turned and raised his hands with his palms pushing towards the small crowd like an incompetent crossing guard, his face reddening, and his eyes wide with concern. "Now there's no reason to get involved here. Let's please move along and let me handle this."

The elf rang her bell as loud as the cheap instrument would allow and shouted, "The Jew is okay." Leave him be!"

Before tempers could grow to physical violence, which seemed a certainty, Simon and Lucy approached. Although a very kind man, Simon's height always drew stares and could have an imposing effect on others. Lucy's dark beauty, assertiveness and verbal fierceness always attracted attention.

"That's enough! Tis the season, after all," shouted Lucy. Everyone looked at Lucy and then up at Simon, who stood quietly staring down at the bigoted individual with a serious expression that had a menacing affect. There was some murmuring and then the group dispersed.

The assistant manager approached Lucy and said, "Thanks to you and your boyfriend, a difficult situation has been averted."

Simon looked down and replied with the deepest voice he could summon, "Let them be."

"I suppose we can make one exception this time," replied the assistant manager before he turned and quickly disappeared inside the mall.

"Thank you," said the elf.

The mime smiled through his beard and clutched his hands near his chest in a gesture of love and gratitude. Simon pulled a hundred-dollar bill from his billfold and deposited it in the elf's bucket, wishing her and the mime a happy holiday.

Once inside the mall, they walked to the food court where they purchased lunch at Stan's Burgers.

"Are you now my boyfriend?" asked Lucy.

Simon considered the import of what Lucy said. He thought about all the short relationships he had had and never considered any of them girlfriends. He enjoyed his time with each woman he had known and was sad when the relationships ended and always initiated by the woman who wanted more of a commitment. There was never any acrimony, as his kindness allowed for a gentle parting. In fact, he, and most of the women he knew continued to exchange annual birthday and holiday cards. Now, he was faced with the 'boyfriend' question.

"It's something we could work on."

"Ah, a working relationship then," said Lucy with an insouciant smile.

They ate their lunches with their usual styles: Simon dripping secret sauce like a coonhound and Lucy nibbling with the neatness of a songbird. Once Simon had finished his burger, fries, and vanilla shake and Lucy had consumed half of her lunch before pushing the remainder aside, Simon remarked, "You were pretty assertive out in front."

"I'm Israeli and most of my family still lives there. I don't have any tolerance for antisemitism. And less tolerance for those who stand idly by."

"Did you serve in the Israeli military?"

"No, we moved to the States when I was very young. My parents have dual citizenship and found better opportunities here."

"Well, you've got gumption."

"It's easy with a tall man at my side. And your silent glare was probably more powerful than my shouting."

"You mean speak loudly and carry a big stick."

Lucy laughed. "I get the reference and you've already figured out that softly isn't in my vocabulary. I guess you are my 'big stick,' though."

As they stood to leave the food court, the elf approached. She wore her costume, but Lucy noticed she wasn't wearing her conical elf's cap. Unlike most bell ringers, she was young and pixyish. Her green elf jacket highlighted her green eyes. She wore her red hair short, like an early Beatle.

"Thanks so much for helping. I had no idea that my boyfriend would cause such a disturbance."

Simon asked, "Your boyfriend is the rude person who verbally assaulted the mime."

"No, the mime is my boyfriend. He thought it would help me to raise more money."

"The mime is your boyfriend," confirmed Lucy.

"Yes, we met through our temple's singles group."

"And you volunteer to be a bell ringer?" questioned a surprised Lucy.

"We're a very liberal congregation."

Simon listened with a bemused expression. His initial reaction to the elf's appearance was noticing that they both shared red hair and that hers was much more stylish than his own. Looking down on the elf gave him a view of perfectly brushed hair parted in the middle. He found the elf to be terribly cute and something of a mismatch to the mime. His kindness allowed him to accept the oddities of any romance. He wondered how often elves and mimes partnered.

"My name is Simon and I'd like to meet your mime."

Lucy looked surprised, her eyebrows raised, and her mouth opened slightly as though she had something to say without yet having formed a thought.

"I'm Lettie and I'm sure Kevin would love to meet you. He's covering for me at the moment, but we'll be finished in about an hour. How about if we meet by the Cookie Palace after we're done?"

Lettie walked away and Lucy turned to Simon and asked why he wanted to meet the mime. Simon told Lucy that he'd always been fascinated by mimes and thought he might want to learn a bit of the craft.

For the next three months, Simon and Kevin met several evenings a week for a couple of hours. At first, Kevin wondered why Simon was so interested in miming. Simon explained that he had been a tall, ungainly, and supremely uncoordinated kid and that it was only recently that he rediscovered basketball with a group of men who called themselves "Rabbit Survivors."

"After a youth spent wanting to be a shorter person, I've found purpose and comfort in my height. For the longest time, I walked with a pronounced slump. When my parents died suddenly, I went into a hermit-like existence. Then my aunt, my only other living relative, passed and my good friends Shel and Goldie…well, really Goldie…goaded me to stand straight and 'get out and live for a change'. When I saw you and Lettie that day in front of the mall, your miming resonated with me. Something about silent movement connects with who I'd like to be."

"What is that?" asked Kevin.

"Expressive with fluid and coordinated movement."

"I think you might just understand what being a mime is all about," said Kevin.

The first month, Kevin coached Simon how to act being trapped in a box. He encouraged Simon to master what he believed was the most basic example of miming.

"We define a physical space by forming imaginary walls and

simultaneously inviting the audience inside our emotional space. Sometimes we even create a door for a more formal entrance and exit."

Kevin always instructed dressed in a black unitard, white gloves, a mask of white makeup with eyebrows drawn in an exaggerated arc, and bright red lipstick, which broadened his narrow lips.

"We wear a mask and gloves to help accentuate our movements and story we are telling. We use those visual props to better convey our silent meanings. I'll get you a proper costume once you've mastered four basic routines: the box, fishing, and toreador."

"What's the fourth?"

"We'll save that as a surprise."

In the beginning, Simon insisted on paying Kevin for the lessons. However, Kevin refused. He explained that his regular job as an automobile mechanic afforded him a comfortable life.

"I'm not a professional actor, Simon. I do it for fun and infrequently in public. Lettie and I do a few charity events and, of course, the annual bell ringer fundraiser."

Simon worked seriously on each routine. Under Kevin's tutelage, he became proficient at defining the walls of an imaginary box with precision and clear definition. Each hand movement carefully placed while his entire body gave the impression of being trapped behind an invisible wall. Once he mastered the box, Kevin had him construct a door.

"You must always open the door by turning the doorknob in exactly the same place each time you enter or leave. Be sure to keep your facial expression neutral and wear your happy or sad mask judiciously. Try entering the room, turn to the audience, and express what happens after a gust of wind slams the door shut."

Simon labored for a week over that complex maneuver. When he had mastered it to Kevin's exacting standard, he began another challenge.

With each session, Simon's confidence grew. He began to feel comfortable with his ability to control his height. He still played Saturday basketball with his fellow Rabbit Survivors, and they began to take note of his improving skills. Simon no longer hung around the hoop for easy lobs and baskets. Now, he moved without the ball and even tried dribbling.

One day he told Kevin, "I'm feeling more at one with my body. I can't thank you enough for all you are doing for me."

After learning the box, fishing and the toreador came quickly. Kevin had him use all three routines to build a short show. Simon's self-confidence grew to the point where he began to extemporaneously add movements. When doing the toreador routine, he might switch from being a confident sword and cape fighter to being the bull with horns and a sad expression and back to the torero, who was now a picture of doom and terror.

"I think you are ready for a public performance," stated Kevin.

"Really?" questioned Simon. "I never thought of doing that."

"Just for friends. Perhaps for just Lettie and Lucy."

During the months that Simon learned to mime, he and Lucy continued to frequently see each other. The boyfriend question did not come up, but they were seen by their close friends and even temporary acquaintances as a couple. Goldie remarked on multiple occasions that Simon had finally found a real soulmate.

"You've finally found your beshert, so don't mess it up," urged Goldie.

Shel added, "When Goldie uses Yiddish, you'd better pay attention."

Simon and Lucy were at dinner, not at Stan's Burgers, but at a fancy Italian restaurant. Lucy sipped her chianti while slowly savoring veal piccata. Simon managed to rush through his lasagna without any landing on his just laundered white shirt or the napkin resting on his lap. Although he still ate too fast, miming had seemed to transform him into a neater eater.

"Kevin wants me to put on a little show," said Simon with all the casualness he could muster.

"That's what Lettie told me."

"She did?"

"Yes, she mentioned it when I saw her at the mall the other day. You've really gotten into it, haven't you?"

"There's something about what I'll call a quiet conversation that I find so meaningful. Even though it's performance art, I find it to be more of an internal conversation which I'm allowing others to witness. It's really hard to explain."

Lucy said, "Maybe it's a kind of body poetry."

"Maybe," said Simon. "I find it very difficult to truly understand poetry. It's such an intimate process. I think the poet is really the only one who understands what they have written. So, maybe it's the same with understanding the language of mime. At any rate, we're putting on the show next Saturday."

"You're giving up your basketball game."

"Just this once."

"Well, I'll be there."

Kevin and Lettie's synagogue had a large meeting room that was available after Saturday services. Being a reformed temple, the sabbath allowed for liberal interpretation. In other words, as long as you came to Saturday service, you could spend the remainder of the sabbath however you pleased. When Simon entered the room dressed in his full mime regalia, he was surprised to see Goldie, Shel, a number of folks he did not recognize, and several Rabbit Survivors milling about.

One of the Survivors remarked, "Here's the big guy and he's looking good."

Goldie approached, "Such a mensch. We're proud of you."

"Where's Lucy?" asked Simon who was not quite sure what to make of the small audience.

Lettie came over and assured Simon she was on her way. A few minutes later, Lucy arrived slightly out of breath and carrying a large yellow tote.

"I'm sorry I'm late. I had to pick up a few things on the way over."

"Not a problem. This show of mine is really meant for you. I didn't expect a bigger audience. Now I'm a bit intimidated. The Rabbit Survivors pose a risk."

"Oh, they'll be fine. And so will you. Lettie tells me that Kevin is really impressed by how well you've learned to mime."

Lucy sat with the others, her tote at her side, and Kevin introduced Simon. He explained that four routines would be mimed. Simon had been learning three…box, fishing, and toreador…he had no idea what Kevin meant by a fourth. As he mimed each of the three selections he knew, he was able to set aside the question about what Kevin meant by a fourth. He thought it must have been a slip of the tongue.

Simon's audience clapped enthusiastically as he concluded each enactment. The Survivors were polite and withheld any ribbing. Kevin sat with a genuine look of pride like a parent whose child was the star of the school's talent show. Lettie sat next to Lucy and whispered quietly to her at the end of each sketch. Simon was so engrossed in his own performance that he didn't notice any of the audience's reactions. As he finished his three routines, Kevin rose and took center stage and Lucy quickly lifted her tote and disappeared into the women's restroom.

Kevin embraced Simon and asked him to remain with him on stage.

"Let's give Simon another round of applause for a job exceedingly well done. There's a fourth skit that I'm going to ask Simon to mime, and it's not one he's previously prepared for."

Simon stood wondering what could possibly be happening. His usually straight posture assumed a bit of a slump, not noticeable to others but felt by Simon, hearkening back to his adolescence. It was his way of being anxious with uncertainty. He looked down at Kevin with puppy eyes and half-open mouth.

"Lettie and I met Simon and Lucy in front of the town's mall. Lettie in an elf costume and I in my mime's. They rescued us from an assistant manager trying to exercise authority and a bully using abusive language. Shortly after, Simon asked me to teach him the art of miming, and I'm so proud of what he's accomplished so far. Every mime must learn to improvise. It's not something we've worked on, but I'm confident that Simon can perform an extemporaneous routine and I'm surprising him by asking him to do one for us. I'm confident in his ability."

The door to the women's restroom opened as Lucy walked to the stage dressed in an elf's costume. She stood facing Simon. Kevin continued, "Simon, I present you with your elf who will initiate the scene."

Kevin returned to his seat. Simon straightened, cocked his head to one side, smiled and waited. Lucy asked, "Are you my boyfriend?"

Goldie and Shel

All through junior high school, Goldie Rothman attracted the attention of others whenever she walked into a room. It wasn't because of anything she said or did, that would come later along with her reputation for being teasingly blunt and unapologetically sarcastic. No, it was because she was the tallest student in her class. Not simply the tallest girl, but at six-foot the tallest person. Seventh grade was a time of awkwardness, walking like a newborn alpaca. Eighth grade was the beginning of smoothness: smooth skin, elegant and purposeful walk, and the acceptance of her own uniqueness. It was also the time of her Bat Mitzvah.

While being tall got her looks, being Jewish got her taunts. One boy in particular caused her constant trouble. David sat behind her in English class, where the rows were straight, and the seats assigned. He wore his blond hair short in a military style and showed a constant smirk revealing his silver braces. When Goldie told her mother about David regularly poking her in the back with the point of his pencil and whispering "kike," Mrs. Rothman faced Goldie and calmly said, "The next time that schmuck does that, I want you to stand up and slap him across the face. And slap him hard."

The next day in the middle of a lesson about persuasive writing, Goldie jumped to her feet and whacked David across the face. She didn't slap; rather it was a full fisted punch. The entire class went numb watching Goldie stand with defiance while David's lower lip trembled with drops of blood oozing. Without any hesitation or request for an explanation, the teacher pointed to the door and directed Goldie and David to immediately report to the principal's office. Goldie led the way, making sure David remained several steps behind.

The principal's secretary instructed them to sit apart on hardbacked chairs. She handed David a tissue to tend to his bleeding lip before leaving and returning with an ice pack, which David now held against his swollen lip. A few tears rolled down his pimply cheek. Goldie sat quietly wondering what was next. She assumed she'd be given a stern lecture and suspended from school.

A bell rang signaling the end of the class period, and a few moments later their teacher walked down the hall and directly into the principal's office. Goldie waited nervously feeling a flush in her cheeks before her teacher opened the door and asked Goldie to enter and sit in the chair across from the principal's desk.

Her teacher leaned over before leaving the office and whispered in Goldie's ear, "You did the right thing. I'll see you in a few days."

Goldie was stunned. She sat rigid wondering what her teacher's words meant. She knew she was going to be disciplined and probably suspended. She did what her mother told her to do, but it didn't feel right. Maybe she should have told her teacher beforehand and not succumbed to violence. Her English teacher was her favorite teacher. It was the only class where she was encouraged to speak her mind. A few years later, when she joined and excelled on the high school's speech and debate team, she always gave credit to her eighth grade English teacher. Now, her stomach hurt and her mouth was dry as she waited for the principal to speak. The 'right thing'?

Shel was intrigued. He had no discernable musical talent, but he loved to hum. Instead of singing in the shower, he hummed. Instead of singing along with hit songs on the radio, he hummed. Walking from class to class, he hummed. Humming and doodling were Shel's two obsessions. When others weren't around, he would hum while doodling. Where other classmates tried to take notes as instructed by their teachers, Shel doodled. His notes were a collection of scribbled pictures, arrows, and symbols which only he understood. On those rare occasions when a teacher would ask to see his notes, they would hand them back and say, "I guess you must know what these mean because you keep acing the tests."

It was an invitation published in the high school newspaper that caught his attention. The music teacher was inviting students to join the Hummingbirds, a coral group dedicated to humming songs. "No musical talent necessary. It's just a lunchtime club for students who want to have fun," said the invitation.

Shel purchased a bean and cheese burrito at the cafeteria, the only school meal he found almost palatable, and walked over to the music room to check out the Hummingbirds. Although short in stature, usually speechless and unassuming in public and private, he was an extroverted dresser Goldie eventually came to describe as "casual serendipity." He entered the music room wearing baggy orange surfer shorts, a loose-fitting Hawaiian shirt featuring a variety of old timey hot rods, and flip-slops that loudly slapped and announced his arrival. He saw three others waiting, including Goldie whom he knew from junior high and their current American government class, a required course for graduation. Sitting apart from Goldie and another girl was David, Goldie's tormentor from eighth grade. Ever since what had become known as 'The Incident' in junior high, Shel, at barely five foot seven, had literally and figuratively looked up to Goldie. He took the seat next to her and began unwrapping his burrito and unscrewing the lid of his water bottle. He noticed that Goldie had a tuna fish sandwich, which she unwrapped from wax paper.

"I don't usually see anything wrapped in wax paper," said Shel.

"My mother refuses to use plastic. She says 'only a mashugana' uses plastic when the world is melting away. Mashugana means crazy."

"I know. It's Yiddish."

"Oh, you're a Member of the Tribe?"

"Yeah. Bar Mitzvah and the whole thing. I never saw you at temple."

"I went to Sholom. You must have gone to Beth El. But I stopped going after my Bat Mitzvah and after I grew up."

Shel laughed, took a sip of water to clear his throat, and said, "I know what you mean."

"So, you're a hummer?" asked Goldie.

"Yeah. It sounds like a club that might be fun. I'm not really a joiner, but I hear the music teacher is a funny guy. How about you?"

"Well, I tried starting my own club, but it didn't work out. Did you hear about the Obsequiens?"

"You mean obsequious?"

Goldie replied, "Obsequiens is my play on the word. It was a club for anyone willing to blindly follow my lead. I thought we might put out a satirical newspaper to counteract the dreck the school paper prints. However, my idea failed for two reasons."

"Two reasons?" inquired Shel.

"First, the school administration said, 'no way'. Second, I had no followers."

"I wish I had known about it," stated Shel.

Goldie and Shel became high school sweethearts. They were inseparable, like mourning doves who hummed rather than cooed. Their affection for one another was public and effusive; they held hands wherever they went and gave each other a quick kiss before departing for classes or other activities. Shel attended every one of Goldie's debate and speech competitions, politely applauding, never cheering out loud when she won, which was most of the time. Shel kept a journal full of pencil sketches of Goldie when she was in the spotlight. One afternoon after a closely fought debate, she asked Shel to share how he had pictured her. His drawing showed her looking like Lady Liberty with her foot planted on her opponent's chest and one arm raised in victory.

"But I lost the debate," said Goldie.

"Not the way I saw it," replied Shel.

Goldie wore a slinky, shiny green dress to the prom, which her mother approved by saying, "Tempting but not a welcome sign." Shel wore his dark blue Bar Mitzvah suit, which still fit. (Fortunately, he did have a slight growth spurt in his senior year, but Goldie still towered over him.) Instead of a traditional shirt and bow tie, he donned an eye-catching orange and yellow Hawaiian shirt and Huarache sandals sans socks. Shel drove up to Goldie's house in his fifteen-year-old, copper-colored Honda Accord, with a scrunched right front fender and a small spider crack in the middle of the windshield. On the way to the dance, Shel learned the full story of Goldie's junior high school suspension, which he had never asked about.

Goldie explained that after she was suspended for fighting, her mother revealed that she had called the principal in advance telling him what she instructed me to do if that creep David kept attacking me with his pencil point and antisemitism. Goldie added that she was still uncomfortable with violence and thought it might have been better if she and her mother talked to her teacher first.

"However, my mother was adamant about me standing up for myself with what she called 'swift and decisive action, like Israel in the Gulf War.' I told her I was a girl not a country. And she told me to 'act more like a country.' The good news is that David has never bothered me again. In fact, he apologized, although I think it was a forced one. He said he was sorry for being a jerk. After the principal had talked to us, his father was the first to arrive. He was one big, scary looking character, with a shaved head and tattoos everywhere. He had swastikas on his neck and arms. He looked at David's swollen lip, glared at me, and I felt a threat that never really went away. My father finally showed up, hugged me and took me home."

"What did your father say?" asked Shel.

"My father is a lovable and very quiet man."

After high school, Goldie and Shel attended community college for two years before enrolling in the local state college. They married at the end of their freshman year, with the encouragement of Goldie's mother, the silent reserve of her father, and the consternation of Shel's parents. It was Goldie's mother who turned to Shel's parents and said, "They're already shtupping enough to make a herd of rabbits, leave the kids alone."

Shel's father, an English teacher at the community college corrected Goldie, "It's a fluffle of rabbits, but what does it matter. Your daughter will make sure Shel follows along."

"She'd better," said Goldie's mother with absolute authority.

The wedding was held at the town's park situated along a pristine lake. Instead of a traditional wedding dress, Goldie wore her slinky prom dress, which her mother said was, "Tempting with a very loud welcome sign." Shel made his own statement in chartreuse surfer shorts, a loud floral Hawaiian shirt, and flip flops. Both Goldie and Shel had convinced their old high school music teacher to have the current edition of the Hummingbirds hum a jazzy version of "Here Comes the Bride" as Goldie was escorted by her tuxedo-clad father down the makeshift aisle. A small reception was held in town at Moshe's Deli, which closed for the private party. A variety of deli sandwiches, salads, matzo ball and cabbage soups, and a sheet pan carrot cake adorned with graphics designed by Shel were served buffet-style. Because Goldie and Shel were still minors, Goldie's mother did not allow for any alcoholic beverages. Toasts were made by hoisting soft drinks, exclusively Dr. Brown's sodas. At one point during the party, David, who was now as large and looking as menacing as his father, but without any noticeable tattoos, walked by the deli, paused briefly, and peered inside without any of the celebrants noticing him.

Shel's parents owned a small apartment house, and, as a wedding present gave them the use of a furnished two-bedroom unit until graduation, while asking them to manage the ten-unit building. Goldie's parents gifted them linens and kitchenware. After graduation, they decided to remain in their cozy apartment and began paying an affordable rent along with the continuing responsibility as managers. Little did they know that they would eventually inherit the property and make it their permanent home, which they enlarged by combining their apartment with the adjacent one-bedroom apartment. They were able to create a spacious home of three bedrooms, two baths, and an open kitchen, dining, and living room. They also renovated the entire building, including each of the remaining eight apartments as they became vacant and available. With increased rents, they lived virtually rent-free. The only tenant who remained was Simon. He was the only person in the building taller than Goldie and the three of them had become close friends. He was someone Goldie also viewed as a "project."

She told Shel, "He needs a life."

"I know you'll make sure he has one," said Shel with no hint of sarcasm.

Goldie graduated with a degree in communications and Shel with one in graphic arts. Goldie joined a small public relations firm and told her friends she was in the "image control business." Shel worked as an independent contractor. He managed to pick up a few clients while in school and positive word-of-mouth kept him busy. He worked from home while Goldie was out "saving egos and reputations." When they weren't working, they took long walks and often had dinner at Moshe's. Goldie's mother patiently waited for a grandchild.

"You two kids are always holding hands or cuddling. Are you sure everything else is working properly? Maybe you ought to go to shul more often."

That's the one thing Goldie and Shel didn't do. They adored their culture but found no worth in being religious. They celebrated a Friday night candle and prayer-free sabbath in their own way. Shel enjoyed roasting a chicken with potatoes and root vegetables crisping in the residual fat. Each week he baked a challah, which made for maple syrup-drenched French toast with thick slices of bacon for Sunday breakfast. They enjoyed routines, reminding them of their childhoods, although bacon was certainly not part of their youth.

Goldie's mother remarked with a bit of a sneer, "Next thing you'll do is make BLT sandwiches on that lovely challah bread. Such a shanda!"

"Mom, it might be a shame, but it's a tasty one."

Both of their parents urged them to at least attend High Holy Day services. "We'll pay," offered Goldie's mother. "You don't have to believe in anything, just show up and make your father and me happy."

The one time they went as a married couple, they sat in the back of the synagogue surreptitiously munching on peanut M & M's. Goldie leaned over and whispered in Shel's ear, "If there is a Jewish hell, I think we've just gained admittance." After services, they were expected to go to a break-the-fast supper which alternated between their parents' homes each year. They never fasted but always attended the dinners.

The news that Temple Shalom had been set on fire early one Saturday morning and almost burned to the ground shook the entire town. The increase in nationwide anti-Semitism had arrived in Bear City, which prided itself in liberal politics and thought itself immune from overt discrimination. Goldie's mother phoned and told her the horrible news. It was one of the few times Goldie heard distress in her mother's voice.

"You and Shel must come down immediately. Our community needs to stand as one. The rabbi is asking for a show of solidarity."

Goldie and Shel arrived to see hundreds of townsfolk clustered in small groups, holding hands, and silently waiting for some direction.

Television and other news media were attempting to interview those in attendance but found no one willing to speak. It was as though the solemnity of the moment rendered everyone speechless. The air was remarkably still and free of smoke and any scent of fire. The sky was cloudless and seemed to be a deeper blue than most days. Standing before the shell of Temple Shalom were Rabbi Rosenthal, the priest from Saint Mathews Church, several other clergy, and the imam from the mosque outside Bear City, since the town had no mosque of its own. The religious leaders stood arm-in-arm, swaying against one another, and faced the increasing crowd with silent prayerful poses. Goldie and Shel found their parents. They all hugged and Goldie felt her mother shudder in her grasp.

"Mom, this is horrible. I didn't think this would ever happen here."

"Goldie, this happens everywhere. None of us is immune from evil."

Once it appeared that all who might come were there, Rabbi Rosenthal addressed the group. He thanked everyone for their kindness and concern. He spoke briefly about the widespread growth of bigotry and the need to include all affected voices in meeting the challenges presented by hate. His sonorous voice evoked authority and compassion and helped to calm the anger and fear felt by those assembled. He made it clear that their work in the days ahead would be far more important than the single action taken against them.

Goldie and Shel stayed until people began to disperse after Rabbi Rosenthal spoke. As they walked back to their car, Goldie noticed David standing on a corner at the end of the block. She bent into Shel and felt tears well.

Barry Vitcov lives in Ashland, Oregon with his wife and exceptionally brilliant standard poodle. His poetry and short stories have appeared in a variety of publications, including: *EAP: The Magazine, Literary Yard, The Scarlet Review, Fiction on the Web, Labyrinth, Mobius Blvd., Black Sheep, Dark Horses, Jefferson Review,* and *The Rapids: An Art & Literature Journal of Southern Oregon.* He has had five books published by Finishing Line Press, a collection of poetry, *Where I Live Some of the Time* (2021); a collection of short stories, *The Wilbur Stories & More* (2022); a chapbook collection of poems *Structures* (2024); a novella *The Boy with Six Fingers* (2025), and a poetry chapbook *Boychik Poems* (2026).

www.ingramcontent.com/pod-product-compliance
Lightning Source LLC
LaVergne TN
LVHW090520110826
845146LV00003B/936